Finding Melody Sullivan is a must-read. Roth... multifaceted narrative of a teen-aged girl navigating friendship, identity, family, and grief, in the context of witnessing military occupation. Rothchild treats all her characters with respect and compassion, and the result is a deeply human story which is, at turns engaging, humorous, surprising, and always honest and authentic.

—Jen Marlowe, author, playwright, filmmaker

The death of Melody's mother leaves a sense of loss that feels dragged deeply into her body. With a father unable to bridge the distance between them, adrift in his grief and on his own mission, she is persuaded to travel to Israel and finds herself left to her own devices, succumbing to relentless waves of fear and loneliness…Hebron becomes her destination and pulses quicken as we encounter military interference, decisions and whims both angry and reckless... The author captures images of refugee camps, blindfolded children, tear gas attacks, rooftop tanks of fresh water but there is a sweetness also in discoveries made as the story moves against the flow of the confused rhetoric she had been used to, and she searches out an understanding and a sense of her own apparent privilege.

—Duncan Lyon, *Sand Paper Stone*

Rothchild has an uncanny ability to honor clashing voices and values – she is pitch perfect in capturing adolescent moodiness and snark, the fearmongering that drives Zionist militancy, the real-time agony that corrodes the life of Palestinians living under Occupation. Lest this all sound like a novel too heavy to read, the story is told with the humor, sometimes just witty, sometimes sly, that teenagers bring to the conversation. It is, above all, a novel about the courage we must find in ourselves to keep hope alive in the impossible world we have inherited. I hope to meet Melody, Yasmina and Aaron again in a few years."

—Eve Spangler, *Understanding Israel/Palestine: Race, Nation, and Human Rights in the Conflict*, Associate Professor of Sociology, Boston College

In this sensitively told story, Rothchild weaves a tale of overcoming grief and discovery during a crucial time in her young protagonist's life. Rothchild gracefully moves through this young girl's profound pain, layering her storytelling with her fragile character's struggles as she reconciles her loss and uncovers the truth about family, friendship, and the broader conflict in the world she encounters. The young characters in her story have something to teach us.

—Paul Zarou, *Arab Boy Delivered*

The colors that Alice Rothchild uses to illustrate the various strands of life in Palestine/Israel are reminders of a stunning piece of Palestinian embroidery. Her intersections of life in Palestine/Israel are clear and vibrant. Through the relationships and experiences of three young people, she brilliantly illustrates the Palestinian/Israeli conflict, revealing to us the humanity behind the politics. It takes the deep understanding of someone who is sensitive towards all the players in that conflict, to write such a touching story that would resonate with the younger generation – and possibly stimulate their questions. As a Palestinian and an educator, I would strongly recommend it to my friends, both young and old, and to teachers of the Social Sciences. It is a heartwarming and truly revealing story.

—Huda Giddens, Founder of the Giddens School, Seattle, WA

Finding Melody Sullivan reminds us that young people have within them the wisdom, instincts and desire to connect and heal across difference in ways that grownups can't figure out. By crossing borders against the grain, hateful tropes are upended to be sources of empowerment. This book reminds us that cross-religion relationships allow us deeper access to ourselves and each other--a timely reminder for a generation saddled with tikkun olam, repairing our broken world.

—Rabbi Alissa Wise

FINDING MELODY SULLIVAN

a novel by **Alice Rothchild**

Cune

Finding Melody Sullivan
by Alice Rothchild
© 2023 Alice Rothchild
Cune Press, Seattle 2023

Library of Congress Cataloging-in-Publication Data

Names: Rothchild, Alice, 1948- author.
Title: Finding Melody Sullivan / by Alice Rothchild.
Description: Seattle : Cune Press, 2023. | Summary: While in Israel,
    sixteen-year-old Melody Sullivan navigates the grief of her mother's
    death and the trauma of a sexual assault, but when she travels to
    Palestine to see her best friend Yasmina, she is forced to face her
    internal demons and the external realities of war and occupation.
Identifiers: LCCN 2022045953 (print) | LCCN 2022045954 (ebook) | ISBN
    9781951082376 (trade paperback) | ISBN 9781614579007 (epub)
Subjects: CYAC: Grief--Fiction. | Rape--Fiction. | Friendship--Fiction. |
    Identity--Fiction. | Jews, American--Israel--Fiction. |
    Muslims--Fiction. | Jerusalem--Fiction. | Palestine--Fiction.
Classification: LCC PZ7.1.R7616 Fi 2023 (print) | LCC PZ7.1.R7616 (ebook)
    | DDC [Fic]--dc23
LC record available at https://lccn.loc.gov/2022045953
LC ebook record available at https://lccn.loc.gov/2022045954

Bridge Between the Cultures (a series from Cune Press)

Afghanistan & Beyond	Linda Sartor
Congo Prophet	Frederic Hunter
Confessions of a Knight Errant	Gretchen McCullough
Empower a Refugee	Patricia Martin Holt
Nietzsche Awakens!	Farid Younes
Stories My Father Told Me	Helen Zughaib, Elia Zughaib
Apartheid is a Crime	Mats Svensson
Arab Boy Delivered	Paul Aziz Zarou

Syria Crossroads (a series from Cune Press)

The Dusk Visitor	Musa Al-Halool
White Carnations	MusaRahum Abbas
East of the Grand Umayyad	Sami Moubayed
The Road from Damascus	Scott C. Davis
A Pen of Damascus Steel	Ali Ferzat
Jinwar and Other Stories	Alex Poppe

 Cune   Cune Press: www.cunepress.com | www.cunepress.net

To Lubna Alzaroo, colleague, friend, and honorary daughter.

Chapter One

CAMEL IN A BACKPACK

MELODY GAZED OUT THE WIDE WINDOW OF her favorite diner, The Buttered Biscuit, as an orange-bellied towhee foraged in the thick shrubbery and the earthy smell of old coffee drifted over her face, reminding her of the pile of unwashed mugs her dad had left in the sink. Her dense red curls were squashed by a black baseball cap, the visor on backwards. "Yaz, my dad said that bird is on some endangered list. Did you know that?"

Yasmina popped a loud pink bubble and tucked a stray hair into her blue hijab. A rim of sweat had collected on her forehead, and the black kohl lining her brown eyes glistened.

Melody rolled her basketball, sticky wet with cut grass, across the table.

"Don't be gross." Yasmina grabbed a paper napkin to wipe the green Formica surface. "Just cause I'm older, doesn't mean I have to clean up after you."

"Thanks, Mom." The words slipped out before Melody could stop them. Instinctively, her fingers went to the fading pink scars on her wrist. She always expected them to be red and raw, a screaming billboard for her grief. Yasmina's eyes narrowed as she watched Melody trace the raised bumpy lines. She opened her mouth to say something, but before she could, Melody preempted her. She wasn't in the mood for Yasmina's pity. Or understanding.

"That bird's just like me, endangered." Melody meant to sound flippant, but instead it came out sounding pathetic, like a bird with a broken wing. The two friends stared across the table. A tense silence.

The ball bounced onto the faux leather seat, and Yasmina wedged it against the wall as the smell of fried onions and sizzling bacon wafted into their faces. The speckled Formica counter across from their booth was lined with customers and steaming cups of coffee. A multileveled plastic display of pies turned slowly near the cash register.

Melody folded her hands into her lap. Thoughts unfinished, as usual. Sometimes she felt so broken, so unfixable, even Yaz couldn't help her.

The waitress hustled over with their food. "Okay, darlins, that's two Cokes, one diet, one regular, one cheeseburger, tomato on the side, one doughnut."

Melody nodded. "Thanks." She frowned as she spotted a tall, gangly teenager peeking from behind the waitress. Aaron. "Fuck." Melody reached for her cheeseburger and whispered, "Mr. Not-so-cute is here again." *Like an annoying brother who won't leave me alone.*

"Hello, lover boy." Yasmina popped another bubble, wrapped her gum in a paper napkin, and slid the doughnut toward her side of the table.

Aaron winced, then cleared his throat after the waitress disappeared. "Hi." Awkward silence. He slid his hands into the pockets of his jeans and shifted uncomfortably from side to side, the cuffs too short, exposing white socks. His eyes were framed by black glasses.

Yasmina smiled. "Are you stalking us or something?"

Aaron blushed and waved his hand. "Oh, no, no. Really no."

"Well what's up?" Melody asked, taking a loud slurp of Coke.

Aaron took a deep breath. "Could I join you two? Like for a Coke or something."

Melody side-eyed Yasmina, but her friend slid over toward the window and chirped, "Sure." She patted her hand on the seat, jangling two gold bangles.

God, Yaz is always so, so cheerful. This dork tried to kiss me in fucking preschool and it's been downhill ever since. Should have whacked him with a Lego or something.

The waitress appeared again, ready to take Aaron's order. "I'll have a Coke." He looked at Yasmina. "Not that hungry?"

Yasmina nodded. "The burgers aren't halal."

"And not kosher," Aaron said. "Too bad."

"So we're in the same boat." Yasmina smiled.

Aaron and Yasmina, having this little bonding moment over food. So not in the mood for his klutzy nerdiness. She caught a whiff of his citrusy, sour man-sweat. *That boy is definitely growing up. Note: Keep Thoughts to Self.*

"Don't you get tired of keeping track?" Melody asked. "Eat this. Don't eat that. I can barely keep track of what I had for dinner last night." *Not that my dad has the slightest idea how to cook.* "Kosher? My grandma did that. But my mom, never." She smirked. "Personally, I'm worried about those awful slaughterhouses, so maybe I should just be a vegetarian."

"Wipe that crooked grin off your face, girl." Yasmina said.

"I could go all vege, except for the part about not eating hamburgers." Melody pretend-chomped.

"Hah," laughed Yasmina.

"I know, I know, I'm a shameless carnivore and you two are serious about religion. It's so weird. I just don't get all the rules. Life's already too complicated."

"But I love you anyway," said Yasmina. Suddenly serious, she turned toward Aaron. "You know, Jews and Muslims really have a lot in common. Like us."

Aaron raised his eyebrows. "Are you for real?"

Is Yaz gonna do her religion is a force for good and can unite us speech? Children of Abraham. Blah blah. Oh god, not with Aaron. Better introduce some reality here. "Then there's my dad." Melody rubbed her nose ring. "Catholic, but so not Catholic. That priest abuse shit was the final straw. It's so perverted. Gross."

Yasmina nodded. "Unchallenged power corrupts, wherever."

Aaron's drink appeared and he settled back into the seat next to Yasmina, wrapping his lanky hand around the icy bottle.

Melody thought this would be a great moment to change the topic. She shot Yaz a look.

"Don't you love these old style Coke bottles? So retro." Yasmina grinned.

"Cool." Aaron nodded, slid his kippah back on his head, and leaned across the table. "Mel, I was talking with my mom. She heard about the conference at work, you know about your trip to Israel. All the secretaries in your dad's department are talking. Especially about how you'll be in Jerusalem."

Yasmina clapped her hands. "Isn't that fantastic? We were just chatting about it on our way over here. My dad heard about it at a staff meeting. That's so exciting. Mel, you're finally gonna travel somewhere, get out of this rinky-dink college town. Out of ridiculously small Vermont." Yasmina mooed and snorted. "Where cows are our biggest attraction. Whoo hoo. And to Jerusalem. Wow. You're really lucky."

Melody groaned. "You both know? News spreads fast around here. If you ask me, I'd rather go to some place like…Hawaii. I could just park myself on a beach under a palm tree with a pen and a pad of paper, and avoid traipsing around with my dad. Like his little shadow. He could find an archeological dig anywhere. I'm so not interested." She scooted toward the end of the seat, turned her back to the window, and stretched her legs across the faux leather. "Check this out." Melody wriggled her phone out of her back pocket, scrolled, and handed it to Yasmina.

Aaron craned his neck over the phone.

Great news, Little Mouse. Paper accepted, we're going to the conference. Jerusalem this summer. You'll finally meet Malkah. Love ya. Dad.

"I hate it when he calls me Little Mouse."

"But this is so cool." Yasmina waved the phone.

"But I don't want to go. Traveling with my dad? It's gonna kill me." Melody pouted, pushing her lower lip up in a big frown. "I mean, I kinda would like to see Jerusalem because my mom loved the place. But." She waved her finger in the air. "This is a big but. My dad's such a dork. He really doesn't understand me at all, and I gave up liking him a long time ago."

"Who's Malkah?" Yasmina and Aaron asked at the same time. Aaron's face reddened.

Shit, they're even thinking the same thoughts. Why is he blushing? "Malkah's a cousin I've never met. My dad thinks we're gonna be BFFs but I wouldn't count on it."

"Oh come on. How bad could it be?" said Yasmina. "Do it for your mom. Maybe some wild adventure will get you out of that deep hole where you live."

Melody winced. She hated Yaz bringing up her mom when she was in her hate- everything-about-dad mood. "Unlikely."

Aaron twiddled his fingers, tapping on the table. "So, like I was saying. Jerusalem is a very holy city for me, I mean for Jews."

Yasmina groaned. "Are you for real? Holy for Muslims, don't forget. And Christians."

Melody sat up straight and swung her legs under the table, tilting her head. "Whoa. Ever hear of the Church of the Holy Sepulcher? The Stations of the Cross? Even my dad, the lapsed Catholic, talks about that stuff."

"Right." Aaron nodded slowly.

Melody studied his straight black hair sticking out like firecrackers under his little round kippah, his puppy hands still too big for his body, the faint stubble on his upper lip. *Is he shaving?*

"But it's like the capital of Israel and it means so, so much to me." Aaron touched his kippah.

Yasmina cleared her throat. "You think it doesn't mean something to me too? As a Palestinian? And a Muslim?"

Aaron stared at Yasmina, eyes wide. "Palestine? Does that really exist?"

Yasmina glared at him and then looked out the window. She took a deep breath. "Trust me, I have family in Palestine. It exists."

Aaron paused, scratched the back of his neck. He looked down and rubbed a dangling cuticle on his thumb.

Wish Aaron would just shut up. Why did Yasmina ever let him crash our party?

Yasmina picked up the ketchup bottle and stared at the label as if she had suddenly developed an intense interest in organic tomato concentrate.

"Well anyway, like I was saying," Aaron continued, "I'm really interested in maybe being a rabbi or something."

"You mean you *like* the whole who begat who and how many goats some famous bearded white guy had?" Melody stroked a pretend beard. "If I had any tendencies toward god, I lost that when my mom died. Like if there was really a god I don't think he – or she." She jutted her chin out and raised her eyebrows. "Or they, would let a kid's mom die." Her voice sounded uncomfortably loud. She stopped and eyed her rose tattoo.

Yasmina put down the ketchup, reached across the table, and rubbed her friend's hand. Aaron took a long slurp of Coke and looked down at his fingernails again while Melody exhaled loudly and stared out the window. Uneasy silence. The towhee flitted across the bushes.

"So, a rabbi? Since when?" asked Yasmina, tilting her head. Melody could always count on Yaz to keep a conversation going, smooth things over with anyone, even when they were being a jerk and she felt like punching them.

"The idea is really growing on me. I know you don't get it, but I'm really fascinated with figuring out this whole G-d thing. And what's our job here on planet Earth. And how to deal with evil, like the Holocaust."

Sweet but nerdy. This conversation is way too, I don't know, way too Annoying and Weirdly Serious. "God? No way. I'd rather pray to a tree goddess." Melody clutched her hands in prayer. "Or a tree frog." She croaked and crossed her eyes.

"Come on, Mel. There's so much unfair and evil in the world, but I feel I have a sense of direction…and a community." He looked straight at Melody for the first time. "It could help you too."

Melody rolled her eyes and turned away. *That's all I need, someone else trying to save me from myself.* "My dad calls religion," she said waving her arms theatrically, "'the opium of the masses.'" She strung out the last word until it sounded like maaaaahses. She saw the pained look in Aaron's eyes as she bowed her head in fake prayer. "Look, I already have a therapist, so thanks but no thanks."

Aaron reached for a saltshaker and shook some out on the table, making swirls with his finger. "My mom's sister lives there, in Israel, but you know, we can't really afford to go visit, with my four sisters and my dad laid off and…"

Yasmina sighed loudly.

"You okay?" asked Melody.

"Too much to explain, my little heathen."

"Try me."

"Another time, sweetie."

Melody picked up the juicy tomato slice. "Anyone want this? Squishy. Yuck."

"Are you squirming out of this conversation?" Yasmina said and poked Melody's hand.

Melody groaned. "You know I can't swallow tomatoes like that. Too gross."

"Another challenge for your deep commitment to vegetarianism."

Aaron shook his head and took a slurp of Coke, his Adams apple bobbing up and down as he swallowed. He reached for the slice and slid it into his mouth. "Well, like I was trying to say," he stared directly at Melody. "Would you bring me something from Jerusalem?"

Melody did a double take. "Wait. What kind of something? I can't exactly fit a camel in my backpack."

"I'd definitely pay you back," he added. "I don't know. Maybe a mezuzah or something kinda religious. It would mean a lot to me."

"What's a mezuzah?" asked Yasmina, sipping her Coke.

"You know, Melody," Aaron said. "You've been to my house."

Yeah, after my mom died…when everyone was trying to feed me. And my dad. Melody licked some of the melted cheese off her bun. "His mom fed us a lot. It's kinda what Jews do. I mean when someone dies."

Aaron nodded in agreement.

"My dad always says, when things are bad, Jews eat, Irish drink," Melody said.

Yasmina smiled. "What does he say about Muslims?"

"No idea." Melody wrinkled her freckled nose. "I guess I should ask him."

"A mezuzah. It's a little box that you nail to your doorway; it has verses curled inside," said Aaron. "Written on parchment paper."

Melody picked up the hamburger bun. "Jews do that mezuzah thing," she said and squirted more ketchup onto the cheese, arranging the sliced pickles in a juicy circle. "Religious Jews, like Aaron," she eyed him across the table, "put them on all their doors." She plopped the bun back on the burger and patted it all together.

"One of our most important prayers, the Shema Yisrael. It's in the Bible, we're supposed to write G-d's words on all our doorposts," Aaron added.

"But what are they *for*?" Yasmina picked up her doughnut, stared at it critically, and took a bite.

"When I walk through a door I touch the mezuzah. It's like saying a quick prayer, checking in with G-d." Aaron gestured, raising his puppy hands, touching an imaginary mezuzah. "They're written with a special quill pen by a scribe. It's really cool."

"I see." Yasmina tilted her Coke and gulped down the rest of the soda, burping as she finished. "So ladylike." She smiled, making a prissy face. "That mezuzah thing sounds nice, actually."

"What do you think, Mel? I'm serious," asked Aaron.

Melody chomped on her cheeseburger as the ketchup exploded from the bun. She dabbed her cheek with her paper napkin. "S'cuse me. Nothing gets between me and my food when I'm hungry. Oh, how I yearn for a French fry." She wiped her chin. "I'll think about it. Something small and meaningful that fits into my backpack and is not a camel. Got it."

She winked at Yasmina as Aaron leaned back in the booth, a smile of relief deepening the dimples on his cheeks. He stretched out his legs under the table and bumped into Melody.

"Oops, sorry." He reddened again.

Melody pulled her feet under the seat; she felt a weird tingling in her body. *What's with him? His feet are way too big for his brain.*

"Excuse me, waitress." Melody waved her arms. "Can I get an order of fries with my burger?"

"Okay doll, back in a sec."

Melody waved her arms again. "Hey, make that a double."

Yasmina touched Melody's arm. "I got exciting news too. In the travel department."

Chapter Two

SWEET AND SOUR

MELODY UNLOCKED THE FRONT DOOR OF HER house and touched her mom's photo propped up on a nearby bookcase, blowing her a kiss. She kicked off her dusty red sneakers and dropped her key on the dining room table cluttered with her dad's student papers and thick textbooks. She stared at the titles, all Archeology, Field Methods, Excavation, Ancient Cities, Jerusalem, The Middle East.

I can't believe Yasmina's visiting her grandma in Israel this summer. Maybe we could travel together, explore someplace really old my mom would have liked. I mean visiting Palestine. She ran her finger over the Jerusalem book. *Sooooo confusing if you ask me. Then Yaz's phone rang and she just bolted out of the diner, leaving me with Mr. Rabbi. So very extremely awkward.*

Melody shook her head and wandered into the kitchen where a large golden retriever was sprawled across the floor. Cheddar opened one eye, snorted, and lifted himself up, padding to the door. Melody leaned over, scratching the dog vigorously behind the ears. "My sweet puppy." He stared at Melody, moon-eyed. She rubbed her face into his fur. "You gonna miss me? Don't worry. Aaron's gonna take care of you while I'm off on my awful Dad adventure." Cheddar licked her face. "We're gonna drop you off at his house. But he'll have the key if you need anything here."

She squatted down next to Cheddar and stared into his eyes. "I can't believe my dad asked him, I mean his mother. She is his secretary, but it's not like doggy day care is in her job description." Cheddar licked her face again. "Of course Aaron said yes. Mr. Helpful. I think I'll put up a NO ENTRY sign on my door, just in case."

"Gotta pee?" Melody let the dog out the back door and sat down at the kitchen table, pushing the breakfast plates to the side, crusted with bits of waffles swimming in calcified syrup. The frozen waffle package lay ripped open on the table, like a half-devoured carcass. She reached for her backpack, draped across a chair. "What a mess. And it's my night to cook. Spaghetti. Again."

Her eyes wandered to an application peeking out from under the pile of unwashed plates, stained by a brown coffee cup ring. Bull's eye. She yanked the paper free. "Summer Poetry Workshop for Aspiring Artists." Parent's signature required. Unsigned. Her father had said something about, "You don't even know where you'll be this summer, Mouse. Why don't you go out with your friends? Do something fun. Don't get so tied up inside yourself." When Melody had scowled, he added, "Your therapist says it would be good if you were more social." She hated when he used her therapist to say what he was thinking. *Had he already suspected we might be going on this mega trip?* She shivered thinking about the fight that followed. In her rage, she had pushed a pile of his papers off the table, scattering them across the dining room floor. He yelled, "Go to your room," his face reddened like an overripe tomato about to burst.

"Too old for that, Dad." Melody just stomped out of the house. *Hadn't he noticed? I'm not a two-year-old having a temper tantrum? I'm a kid whose mother died, for Christ's sake.* She had felt like she was about to shatter into a thousand pieces. All the words in all her poems jumbled, chaotic, blown sky high into the storm. Even now, her heart quickened as she remembered sobbing alone in that deserted park near school, the smell of dog pee adding to her despair, crickets chirping like tiny bursts of gunfire. She had sat there for hours, biting her fingernails, rubbing the bracelet on her wrist, dreading going home to another war of words or frosty silence. Home. War zone.

Be social? My friends? Really?

Melody feared she had used them all up. Except for Yaz, her super-sister. *I mean how many times can someone offer you a box of tissues? Put a sympathetic hand on your shoulder? Listen to all that honking while you blow your drippy nose?* She felt 100%, irredeemably pathetic. She stabbed her finger in the old maple syrup and wrote STUCK in loopy script. Her dad didn't understand, poetry was the tether to her life before, to her grief after. All she really wanted to do was hide in a dark hole and write, all pathos and sorrow. She licked her finger. She loved that word, pathos. It was her kind of word. She stuck her finger back in the syrup and wrote P-A-T-H-O but the S ran into a crusted burnt end of a waffle. She worried that her poems were too whiney and sad, self-absorbed, but it was the only way she knew to get that brooding, tormented stuff out of her. Purge poetry. She felt like she was talking directly to her mom, as if a huge celestial ear hovered over her, absorbing her sorrow. She could feel her mom's presence, a delicate shimmer in the room, listening when everyone else was sick of her.

Her father had become so detached. Sometimes, without warning, he wouldn't come home until late, muttering about meetings and papers. But actual listening, talking with her, not his superpower. Not even on the to-do list. *If it's not in his syllabus, it's not happening.* Melody had taken to making the grocery list every Thursday. Otherwise, he would come home without milk, Diet Coke, Fritos, or double chocolate ice cream. The essential food groups. He hadn't gotten the how-to-take-care-of-a-kid memo yet. Probably never would. That was her mom's job. Now, that job application was lying empty in the middle of her life, just like her poetry course.

She tucked her hand into her pack and searched for a crumpled piece of lined paper, dragging her teeth against her lip, blanching the redness to pale pink. She wished she hadn't eaten all those fries; her belly felt tight against her jeans. She thought about the chocolate chip cookies in the pantry, her go-to comfort food in times of desperation. *If you eat those, you will definitely puke. Don't do it. Besides they're just crappy Heavenly Chips.* She sat up straight and loosened her belt a notch, unbuttoning the top of her pants. *They're like cardboard. Not like Mom's.* Melody loosened her belt another notch. *Mama really knew how to bake a cookie. Lots of semi-sweet chunky chips for starters. Gotta get a bag of those. Put it on the shopping list. Maybe two bags.* She flattened out the paper from her backpack with the side of her palm and started to write.

Sinking into a cavern of loneliness,
Falling, drowning,
Where is my life raft?
My boat?
How will I learn to swim
When you have left me?

Melody stared at her rose tattoo etched around the bumpy scars, the stem woven into a wavy M-O-M. Her silver braided bracelet slipped toward her elbow. Her mind drifted to her mother's cool fingers against her warm palm, the peach fuzz covering her mother's scalp, the breath wafting across her cheek as they lay next to each other. The soft in and out that slowed and slowed like the tide on a quiet, windless evening. She felt enshrouded in the silence around her. Her shoulders slumped against the speckled plastic back of the kitchen chair and the tight muscles in her neck let go. For a moment.

Melody flicked her shiny black fingernails nervously and thought of the tsunami of tears that followed that last long exhale, the fear that the flood she couldn't control would just wash her out to sea. But she was still afloat, bobbing in the waves, swept by the currents, tangled in the seaweed and plastic scraps of her messy life. And her father, just as unmoored.

She bit her nail, the memory still sharp as a dagger. The day she came home from school and found her father standing, red-eyed in the bedroom, like a lone, charred tree still upright after a massive forest fire, surrounded by boxes of clothes, her mother's clothes. Melody stared at the folded sweaters and jeans, the open closet. It gaped back at her like an empty coffin. She remembered the rise of rage and panic, the screaming. "You're a heartless monster. That's what you are. You're packing up her things? Are you trying to get rid of her?" Her father's unfocused stare. Melody grabbed a shirt her mom always wore in the garden and ran to her room, sobbing. When her father appeared at her door, he just stood there. Lost. Silent. Adrift on his own ice floe.

He just glided out to sea. Leaving me, his only daughter, stranded, clutching an old work shirt, still stained with dirt and sweat. Probably covered with her skin DNA. That felt important to save. At least she had the bracelet.

"My dad, the absent-minded, robot professor," she said under her breath. "Even when Mom was alive. Here, but not really *here*. I'm such a fucking orphan. Just look at this place." Her gaze swept over the sink, still piled with last night's dirty pots. "This place needs a mother. Or at least a father-mother." She ran her finger under the braided silver band around her wrist and gently kissed the three emeralds set in the silver. She looked across the room to the photo near the door. "Mom. It's like you're watching over me, holding me. And I'm just hanging on."

Melody reached for her phone and skimmed slowly through old photos. Three years ago, there was her mom, stirring pea soup on a frigid winter evening, her coffee-colored eyes crinkled in a smile, framed by a mane of curly brown hair. Melody remembered the aroma of freshly baked bread permeating the kitchen. "Always loved your bread…and your hair. The Mane," she whispered, as if speaking in a hushed voice would bring her mom back from the grave, as if she were communicating with her, ghost to ghost. "You were my lioness." She smiled and growled at the photo. "And I was your cub."

Melody tilted her chair back and stared up at the ceiling, taking note of the paint peeling around the hanging light. Nothing in the house was getting enough love. "Damn it. I hate tears." She wiped her eyes with her sleeve. Her mascara smudged.

She thumbed through more pictures and then stopped. There was her mom, grabbing plastic chopsticks and popping a spicy pork dumpling into Melody's open mouth. They were both laughing as they snuggled together at their favorite Chinese restaurant, goofing for the selfie. Melody remembered that day. Her mom clenching the wheel, white-knuckled, driving Melody to a violin lesson, snow flying sideways. "We can do this, chipmunk." Then sitting with her patiently as she struggled over scales and arpeggios. Stopping at Asian Bistro on the way home, the taste of sour soy sauce and tangy sweet General Gau's chicken. And then the Monster Cancer arrived and devoured everything.

Melody swiped at her phone, each photo popping a visceral memory into her brain, a moment, ethereal but held distinctly in her palm, as if stopping time. She paused at a selfie with Yasmina, both clowning for the camera, blowing giant pink bubbles, just touching the tips of their noses. *I really love that girl. She's my rock. But there's some strangeness about her, like she's holding something back.* Melody looked up from her phone and bit her lip. *Sometimes she looks so…sad, but she won't tell me what's getting her down…*

There was that conversation at The Buttered Biscuit, how Yasmina sidelined some of Melody's questions, just shut down when Aaron started waxing poetic about Jerusalem. *Which brings us to Aaron. What the hell is going on with him? The dork ignored me for what? Ten years.* Melody shook her head, her crazy curls bouncing. *Now suddenly he's skulking around, sniffing at me like a puppy. He's so sincere, but religion? Not my bag.* She dug for her favorite pen. Since her mom died, poetry had become her solace, her own available-anywhere-anytime therapy. She fantasized being a writer someday, winning fancy poetry awards, the big twitter account, thousands of Instagram followers, the slim volumes lining up on her bookshelves. That is, if she could only survive being a teenager. She thought getting to twenty would be a total relief.

Shit. Shit. Shit. A wave of nausea and tiredness hit her. She closed her eyes, leaning back into her chair. Her head was heavy, weighted with unrelenting sadness. She played with her bracelet, the emerald stones smooth and comforting. *I feel exhausted. What is wrong with me? Must have been that basketball game with Yasmina. She's damn good.* Melody stared at the grimy dishes. *Maybe I could just sleep through making supper? Dad will probably be late from classes anyway and he's gotta be tired of spaghetti. I definitely am.*

Melody grunted, stood up, and stretched. She shuffled into her bedroom and plopped onto a heap of pillows, then wriggled around and tucked her toes under her mohair blanket, black-painted toenails disappearing beneath the pale green wool. Pulling the soft, scratchy cover close to her face, she inhaled the faint salty sweetness. "Still smells like you, Mom." She ran her finger under the braided silver band around her wrist and rubbed the emeralds with a slow, hypnotic rhythm. Her body floated, detaching, drifting, the day rewinding in her head. She sank into the pillows.

In her dream, she felt herself slow-motion falling, flailing down some mossy well, filled with snakes and frogs, leering, cackling, and blowing rancid breath in her face. She tried grasping the slimy rock, but the skin tore from her fingers. Suddenly, she splashed into deep icy water, frantically dogpaddling, coughing, choking. From the corner of her eye, she spotted a thick rope dangling in front of her. She looked up. Far above her, she could see a circle of light and agitated faces, worried, staring, calling her name as it echoed toward her. Aaron was yelling the loudest, "Melodeeeee," and waving a mezuzah. Cheddar was with them, barking desperately, orbiting around the well in a frenzy. She hurled herself toward the rope, grabbed it, but couldn't get a grip on its slippery surface and fell back into the water with a massive, shivery splat.

Melody jolted awake, her heart thumping. "What the fuck was that?"

Cheddar barked at the backdoor, dragging Melody into reality.

Chapter Three

AT RISK

MELODY CATAPULTED DOWN THE COURT AND sprang into the air, tossing her basketball through the hoop with a swoosh.

"You go girl." Yasmina came in close behind her and swatted at the ball midair. The two girls dodged each other, back and forth, their feet dancing across the court, trickles of sweat dripping down their sides.

"That's nine for ten," yelled Melody. "I'm so gonna beat you this time."

Yasmina whooped and laughed as she dribbled down the court. Melody flailed her arms in Yasmina's face, bouncing up and down, red sneakers streaking after her friend. She swooped across Yasmina's body, grabbed the ball, and tore down the court toward the grassy edge. The ball arched upward and plunked into the hoop again.

"Game," shouted Melody, pumping her fist. She dribbled off the court. "Thanks, big sister. Can you handle it? Water?" Melody squatted at her pack and pulled out a plastic water bottle.

Yasmina grabbed it and chugged. "I don't know, defeat is so painful," she said, raising her eyebrows. "Wanna sit?"

Melody nodded and they collapsed onto the grass.

Melody pulled her knees up to her chest and stretched out her back. She heard a loud crack. "Ouch." She could feel her tee shirt, drenched with sweat, stuck to her body.

Yasmina extended her legs and pointed her toes skyward. "Ahh," she groaned. "My calves. I should stretch more. You know, it's not really fair that you beat me so often, cause your legs are so much longer than mine."

"My goal was always to keep up with you, Yaz. You've always been my superhero, I mean super-heroine." Melody smiled, placed her hands over her heart, fluttered her eyelashes, and giggled. "Feels good to laugh about something for a change. My dad is so pissed at me. My general lack of enthusiasm, not to mention that D in Chemistry." She closed her eyes and snorted loudly. "Why should a poet have to know what an oxider is anyway?"

Melody's voice deepened and she crunched her eyebrows together. She waved her finger in the air. "I just can't believe that my daughter, the daughter of a professor at such an esteemed college, could do so badly in school." She hung her head in mock shame. "Such a terrible waste of talent. And intellect." She leapt up and pretend-strangled herself, making choking gasps, and then collapsed on the grass, laughing. "Help, I'm losing my electrical charge."

Yasmina handed her the water bottle, a big grin on her face. "Stop. Drink. You know dehydration is a serious health hazard."

"Yes, Dr. Yaz." Melody chugged as water dripped down her chin. "Thanks for the H-2-O. Who would have thought we would still be friends, after all this time?" She started singing the good morning song from preschool.

Yasmina hummed along. "The bonds forged over potty training are forever. I taught you everything you know," she said playfully. "Plus seriously, I think I kind of adopted you when your mom got sick."

Melody nodded and felt a lump rising in her throat. The light-hearted goofiness in her body sank toward her toes.

"You feeling sad?"

Melody sighed. *Gawd, a dead mom is forever. I am so endlessly obsessed with death.* She lay down on the grass, stared at the clear sky, and rubbed her finger along her silver bracelet, stopping at the smooth surface of the emeralds.

"Are you worried about the trip with your dad? It might be an opportunity, shake up your life in a good way." Yasmina's eyes got real serious, like she could almost see inside Melody's despair. "You've been down so long. It's been a year, right? Since she died?"

Down a dark hole, into the dank, mossy well of her dream. Melody's mind drifted to that awful evening, the smooth, cool feel of her mom's sharp sewing scissors, the curious pressure on her wrist. She hadn't felt anything but a sense of surprise at the warmth of her blood. Like a dark, red trickle. No pain. Until it was all over. Her dad's horrified face. The rush into the bathroom, her dad grabbing a towel, the pressure on her wrist, carefully steri-stripping the cut when the bleeding stopped. Then dragging her to the shrink with the dark blue eyeliner and beaded earrings. "Melody, I think this is a cry for help. We can work on this together."

Yasmina's sharp voice penetrated her memories. "Mel, I'm talking to you. You there?"

Melody jolted into the present and sat up, hugging her knees. Briefly, her mind danced around. *What's gonna kill me? Plane crash? Large truck? Breast cancer?* "They say daughters are at risk. What the hell does that mean? At risk." She stared down at her toes and wiggled them back and forth, the ends of her red sneakers rippling. Blood red.

"What are you talking about?

"Oh, forget it."

"Really? Little sister, this sounds serious. Are you afraid of…"

"Yaz, have you ever lost someone you really cared about?"

Yasmina stared at Melody. Silence. "Yeah, I had a cousin, Ibrahim, he was one of my favorites," she said softly.

"What happened?"

Yasmina took a deep breath and opened and closed her hands. The twinkle faded from her eyes. "He got shot."

"Holy Jesus, shot? How?" Melody sat up and touched Yasmina's shoulder.

"You know. Wrong place, wrong time. Israeli soldiers. It was years ago. He was just a little boy coming home from school. But I loved him."

"I'm so sorry. You never told me."

Yasmina nodded.

"Then you kinda know what I'm feeling. This gnawing in my heart that never goes away."

Yasmina squeezed Melody's hand. "Mel, I have something to tell you."

Melody tilted her head and looked at Yasmina.

A serious look passed over Yasmina's face. "You know I told you I'm gonna travel this summer. My dad says I'm going home."

"Home? Isn't this home?"

"I mean home to Palestine, to visit my fam, in Hebron. My grandma's kinda sick and my dad wants her to see me, maybe for the last time."

"That sounds serious."

"Yup. I'm really afraid of losing her, before I really get to know her in person. But I'll also get to see my cousins, like *a lot* of cousins, which should be fun. And of course, I think my grandma is dreaming that she can find me a fiancé, some nice traditional Muslim boy from Hebron or some nearby village, so that should be interesting. Can you believe it? She thinks seventeen is too old to be single."

"Yikes."

"Yikes is right. I haven't been there in five years. I mean we talk every week, but this is different."

"That's good that you'll visit, especially if she's real sick. But I can't see you betrothed quite yet." Melody grinned and fluttered her eyes and held out her left hand, ready for a ring. "The shy groom, his sophisticated American bride. Long white dress. Popping pink bubbles, obviously. Does anyone speak English there?"

Yasmina rolled her eyes. "Yes, of course. And weddings are ginormous and go on for days. So that's not my style either."

"Jeez, like they kill a sheep or something?"

Yasmina nodded. "Maybe even two sheep." She laughed. "And two goats."

Suddenly Melody's mood shifted, and she felt excited. "Then we can meet in Jerusalem when I'm there. You can show me around. Right, Yaz? Show me all those ancient places my dad's always talking about. Hey, maybe we could go swim in the Dead Sea together. I hear it's incredibly salty and…"

Yasmina lowered her eyes. "Well, maybe. My uncle says it's much harder to travel now. I'm not sure, so maybe, maybe not. I gotta go see for myself."

"What do you mean, maybe not…see for yourself?" demanded Melody, slapping one hand on her hip.

"It's complicated."

"Complicated?" Melody stuck out her chin and frowned. Her mood torpedoed abruptly.

"Look, I'll talk with my dad and he'll talk with my uncle and see what's possible. I've…I've never actually been to Jerusalem."

"Never? Are you talking in some kind of code? What do you mean, what's possible? Isn't everything in the so-called Holy Land like real close together? Don't you go pray at some big mosque there?"

Melody stuffed her curls under her baseball cap and shoved the visor downward over her forehead. Her knee jittered with sudden anxiety. Her Holy Land escape plan was going down the tubes.

"Yes but, Mel," Yasmina stopped and took a deep breath. "My family can't just hop in a taxi or a bus and bop off to Jerusalem."

"Why not?"

"We need permits."

"Permits?" Melody peered out from under her visor, confused. She knew about permits to leave school early or go to a national park or learn to drive a car, but permits to get on a bus?

"We have to get through checkpoints and military terminals. My uncle is a journalist, and he's on security lists. Like I said, it's complicated."

"But wait, you're an American citizen. Girl, you were born in the US. Why can't you just go anywhere, like me?" Melody's face flushed, freckles popping, her voice growing loud.

"Because it's complicated," Yasmina said. A hardness crept into her tone. "When I'm there, my US citizenship doesn't matter much. I'm a Palestinian. I can't even use the same airport you use."

"That's fucked up!" Melody exclaimed and grabbed a small rock, throwing it against a nearby maple tree with a loud whack.

"There's a lot of weird things and I'm afraid it is getting weirder," Yasmina answered, eyebrows tented up. "But like I always say, keep on…"

"Marching forward, I know, I know." Melody snorted and frowned.

The girls sat quietly, thinking. A chasm of misunderstood realities split Melody's thoughts. She couldn't imagine her Yasmina stuck somewhere, unable to travel. What was a checkpoint anyway? She looked at her friend; she seemed distant, drifting toward another planet. Planet fucked-up-where-nothing-Melody-took-for-granted-could-be-counted-on. Melody pulled up a thin blade of grass, then another and another, and twirled each one between her fingers until her thumb took on a greenish hue. She stared up at the sky. *Did they even grow grass there? Was it mostly desert? Camels? Maybe a few cactuses? On Yaz's planet Palestine.*

"I hope you're not trying to mow the lawn. It's not very efficient," said Yasmina. Melody cracked a lopsided smile and blew her a kiss.

Chapter Four

FLYING TO THE PROMISED LAND

ELODY WALKED PAST THE SECURED GATE HOLD AREA sign and entered the waiting room for her flight. She got in line, her dad close behind her.

"Take your shoes off, leave liquids in the backpack," the security agent announced.

"My jacket?" *This is so annoying.* Melody snuck a look at the man. Their eyes met. *Not friendly.*

Her father nudged her elbow.

"Off." The officer briskly peered into her backpack and swept the contents with a wand. He gestured for her to spread-eagle and waved the wand over her body. "Go."

How many times will they screen me? I feel like a criminal. As Melody gathered her stuff, she turned to her father. "Third time, Dad. Boston, Newark, and now this. Fucked up."

Her father raised his thick, copper-colored eyebrows. "Well."

"And each time the rules are different. What's with that?"

Her father exhaled loudly. "Top notch security, Mel. Israelis. Keeps everyone safe. It's just how it is."

"That's not a good enough reason." *Why is my dad dragging me along on this trip? It's not like he's close with my mom's sister or anything.* Melody glared. *He could do his stupid archeology without me tagging along when I'd rather be in my bed, door locked, snuggled on Cheddar. Writing my way out of my life.* She grabbed her jacket. *And his.*

She threw her denim jacket over her shoulder, her Prochoice buttons tapping against Fight Global Warming and Save the Seals, and headed toward a row of seats. Melody stared at a young man, pink cheeked with a scraggly beard, twirling his big black hat on one finger like a Frisbee. She raised her eyebrow, a mix of curiosity and disdain. *God, I hate religion. When did that make the world any better? Everybody's sure they have the RIGHT answer.* She took another quick peek at the bearded young man.

It's such a mess. Like this airport and its bizarro security, not to mention gas guzzling planes. Are we or the planet any safer?

"The departure terminal. Behind a food court? Way at the end of the corridor? Dad? Are you listening to me?"

"I can hear you, Mel. Maybe they're making it hard to find?"

"Really, it's an airport. We're supposed to find things."

"They've got a lot of enemies." Her father stopped to fill his water bottle.

Then why the hell is he taking me there if it's so dangerous? "Dad? SECURED GATE HOLD AREA? That's creepy. What does that mean? The rest of the airport isn't exactly unsecured."

"Sweetie, it's called deterrence. They're being careful." He took a swig of water and wiped his mouth with a white handkerchief that was tucked in his pocket. They approached the seating area for their flight.

"Really? I mean it's not like I could sneak a BOMB into the airport after I've checked in or anything."

Three college students wearing Spartans for Israel tee shirts, a nun, and an elderly gentleman looked up as she uttered the word "bomb". A thirty-something woman in a baggy tunic volunteered, "The world's a dangerous place darlin'. Get used to it."

"I won't get used to it."

"Chill out, honey. It's a long flight." The woman turned back to her *yes!* magazine and flipped the page, straightening the glasses perched in her hair.

Melody wrinkled her forehead, staring at the woman. She could see half the article, the words, "Black Lives Matter," something about protests and justice. *Chill out? So not happening.* She moved down the aisle and plopped next to a family with seven wriggling children. *At least there's some local entertainment. I wish I had a sister. But only one. I mean, there's less-lonely and there's everyone's-always-stealing-your-toys-and-you-have-no-personal-space-less-lonely. I'd friggin' kill myself.*

Her father sat down next to her, placing his leather briefcase between his knees, and took out a *New Yorker* magazine.

Melody scanned the waiting area, "The world's a dangerous place," reverberating in her brain. *Cancer? Plane crash?* She felt a shiver of anxiety down the back of her neck and curled protectively into her seat, then reached into her gray backpack, the FIGHT POVERTY NOT WAR sticker peeling off the back. She pulled out a fresh, new notebook. Her fingers wandered into the pack's inside pocket and felt around her passport until she reached her favorite pen. She doodled a circle of planes, each crashing into the *Sustainable Earth, made from recycled paper* label, opened the notebook to the first blank page, and bit her lip.

Page one

THE WORSTS

1. *Cheddar getting hit by a car and D-Y-I-N-G.*
2. *Sharp sewing scissors.*
3. *Falling in love and then heartbreak: AVOID AVOID ** probably will never happen anyway.*
4. *Phone death – and then Dad making me work to replace my only connection with the universe.*
5. *THE BIG ONE ABOUT TO HAPPEN: Left alone in a strange city, lost, lonely, no friends.*
6. *Getting on a plane to above city: CONSIDER FLEEING TO SAFETY!!!*
7. *Nuclear war and global warming, too grim to worry about now. There is always tomorrow.*
8. *Missing Mom.*

She could feel the thump, thump of her pulse bursting in her head and imagined sitting here with her mom. Alive. Talking. Patting her knee when she felt angry, afraid. Giving her hugs when she got her scared-little-girl look. Her mom would have called this, "The trip of a lifetime." She would have called her, "My little sweet potato," and rustled her ginger hair. They would have sat close, giggling over some private joke.

Shit, we never got the chance at so many things. Melody rubbed her eyes, smearing some mascara off her jet-black eyelashes. She touched her nose ring absentmindedly. "It's so not fair." She looked down at her silver bracelet and imagined it dangling from her mom's skeletal wrist, the three emeralds clunking on the hospital tray.

The day she unclasped it, she said, "Honey, this is for you. Always remember, I love you." Tears surged and Melody squeezed her eyes tight, awash in the memory of the smell of hand sanitizer and lavender soap. Lavender was her mom's favorite. Hospital hand sanitizer was not. The fragrance of lavender always made her cry. Like she could almost touch her. Almost. Like she could inhale her.

Her dad looked up from his magazine. "Did you say something, Mouse? Are you crying?" He bent toward her and took off his wire rimmed glasses.

"Forget it." Melody groaned and turned away, hiding her face, and watched a little kid grab a doll from his younger sister. Melody pulled her arm away when her dad patted her hand. She heard a spasm of shrieking while an older sibling returned the doll and the mother, wearing a wig that was slightly off kilter, rocked a squirming infant. An older woman in a hijab smiled and tried to distract the boy with the letters and numbers on her boarding pass.

A cluster of teens in tight jeans walked by, talking excitedly about Masada and the Dead Sea, when one of them stumbled over Melody's backpack strap. "Oops. Sorreee." The girl grinned.

Melody waved her hand dismissively. *Klutzes.* She spotted several young men in tall black hats and long coats, wispy beards sprouting from their chins, a tight banana curl bouncing off of each shoulder, faces buried in prayer books, rocking back and forth. The kid grabbed the bedraggled doll again. *Maybe being an only child has its advantages. Or maybe being the only person on the planet. No one to bother me. Or trip over my stuff.*

Melody listened to the babble of English and Hebrew, the raised voices, the hum of prayers, the occasional Arabic and Russian, a dash of French. A sparrow frantically flitted between the rows. *This trip better be worth it, little bird.* She curled into her seat and shoved in her ear buds, thumbing through her playlist and rubbing her silver bracelet. Legs crossed, her toe bounced to the soothing twang of "Here Comes the Sun" as she hummed along. Big sigh. *That's the one my mom loved.* Melody sank into the sweet strum of the guitar. "Little darlin'" felt like they were singing directly into her sad and lonely heart, her own cold, cold winter. Her endless search for sunshine. *Thank you, George and Paul.*

Melody leaned back into her seat and stared at her notebook. At the end of her list, she sketched a lopsided daisy leaning on a heart. *Makes me want to play acoustic guitar.* She smiled. *But that would involve practicing. Sorry Mom.* She took a tissue out of her pack, blew her nose and dabbed her eyes.

The kid looked at her with a quizzical expression. "Mah zeh?"

She shrugged and picked up her notebook again.

Page two

Take two.

Is this a new beginning?
Will I find my place?
Dig myself out of this hole?
Expand my horizons?

I am marching along,
Showing up,
Standing in line,
Doing what I'm told.

Melody stopped and looked at her hands, her chipped black nail polish. *Gotta stop with the biting. So unattractive.* She traced her finger over the rose tattoo on her wrist, her bumpy scars entwined in delicate leaves.

But I'm still lost,
Still floating on the wreckage.
Looking for something, someone,
To hold.

Melody put her pen down and closed her eyes. She cupped her hand over her ear and leaned into her ear bud. George Harrison's voice warbled into her brain. Suddenly she heard, "Delta flight boarding now for Tel Aviv. If you have not completed security, please proceed directly to the gate."

"Okay, this is it." She got in line with her dad, behind the clutch of bearded twenty somethings, accidentally brushing against one of the men. He glared at her and moved briskly away. "Sorry." *Men. Religion. Bad combo if you ask me.* Melody smiled stiffly at the attendants as they scanned her ticket, and she headed down the jetway. When she reached the door, she stopped, rubbed her hand against the white metal plane, leaned forward, and kissed it. "Don't crash, okay? I need a chance. Promise?"

"Melody, what are you doing?" her father scolded. "That's not very sanitary. And you're holding up the line."

Melody ignored him and stepped into the plane, scanning the massive interior, the rows of blue screens all standing at attention, the beaming attendants. *They're too perky.* The line crawled down her aisle, passengers stopping to heave bags into the overhead containers. She slid into her seat, 52B. *How can those people smile so much?*

As the flight attendants did their seatbelt/life jacket pantomime, Melody pondered. *What a bizarro job. Is there anyone on the planet who doesn't know how to buckle their stupid seatbelt?* She unsnapped her seat buckle a few times as a personal protest. *Maybe it's all a distraction. This ginormous plane taking off. Not falling out of the sky. Against all the laws of gravity. Just don't think about it.* She unbuckled her seatbelt one more time.

"Melody, please keep your seatbelt on," her dad growled in his exasperated professor voice. Melody rolled her eyes. Snap.

As the engines finally thundered and Melody leaned back into her chair, the smell of fuel drifted into the cabin. She stared out of the window, daydreamy. The runway flitted by and soon stretches of blue waves and then clouds raced past, first wispy followed by a dense swathe of gray-white. "Goodbye life as I know it." She exhaled long and slow, and sang softly, "I'm coming sun, sun, sun, sun, and I'm gonna be just fine."

The clouds turned into a distant haze. Melody thought about everything she would miss back home, and this deep sense of loss dragged into her body. She clicked on her phone and scanned through her photos. Cheddar leaping on her bed. Cheddar galloping in the woods. A goofy close-up of Yasmina sticking out her tongue. A sad selfie, face wrapped in blankets. Like a baby. A sad, sad baby. Her mom standing under a graceful oak tree, laughing. She opened her notebook.

Page three

THE LEFT BEHINDS

1. *Cheddar, (my baby).*
2. *My bed.*
3. *Mohair blanket.*
4. *Basketball court.*
5. *Yasmina.*
6. *Mom stuff.*
7. *Cheeseburgers.*

Melody stopped abruptly. "Hey, Dad. Do they have cheeseburgers in Israel? Is everything kosher there? You can't mix milk with meat, right, Dad?"

"Good question on the cheeseburgers, Mouse," he said, not taking his eyes off his magazine. "I don't really remember, but we're gonna find out. Think of this as our big explore. Like an archeological dig, looking for clues and artifacts. You and me."

Melody took her pen and wrote USELESS over and over again on the rest of page three. *He's like made out of cardboard. I know he has a brain, a professor brain anyway, but is he really human? Does he have a heart?* She drifted into a fantasy of her father as the Tin Man in the Wizard of Oz. With glasses and red hair. "If he only had a heart," she sang softly.

"But I'm definitely not Dorothy," she said definitively.

"Did you say something, Melody?"

"Just forget it."

An attendant with a neatly trimmed beard peered down her row. "Pretzels? Nuts? Soda?"

"Nuts sounds appropriate," she murmured under her breath.

Chapter Five

A VERY LONELY PLANET

Hours later, Melody squirmed in her seat, adjusted her ear buds, and stretched out her long legs, bumping her shins into the seat ahead. *I feel like a frigging pretzel.* A faint trickle of light seeped into the darkened cabin despite the closed shades. "What time is it, Dad?" She nibbled on her fingernail.

Her father stirred, heavy lidded, half asleep. "Boston time? Tel Aviv time? Somewhere over the ocean time?"

"Come on Daddy. I can't sleep," she sighed. "Talk to me." She took off her ear buds, plopped them into her lap, and turned to face him.

Her father clasped his fingers together and stretched his arms forward, working out a kink in his back. "Mouse, it's a long flight."

"Really? I hadn't noticed." She stared at him with a sharply raised eyebrow. "It was long before we even started. And with all that extra security shit and endless waiting..."

"Mouse, we agreed no curse words while traveling. And stop biting your fingernails."

"Okay Daddio. I'll try, try, try." She crossed her arms over her chest and thumped them into her lap. "But how about you try not calling me 'Mouse.' It makes me feel like a fucking rodent."

"Melody!"

"Sorry, Dad." She put her hands together as if she were praying. "I'll try harder."

"Look, this is our adventure. Your mom always wanted us to go, visit her sister, meet the cousins. Let's work on getting along, okay?"

"But Da-ad, you're gonna be in that conference all day. What am I gonna do?"

"Jerusalem's an incredible city, the archaeology is spectacular, and I think you will have fun just...exploring. You love history."

How would you know what I love, she thought darkly.

He reached under the seat and opened his briefcase. "I got this for you. I've highlighted the places in the Old City I think you would like." He handed her a copy of the *Lonely Planet, Israel & the Palestinian Territories Travel Guide.*

Melody harrumphed, grabbed the book, and put her ear buds back in. "It's so impossible to have a real conversation with you. I already live on a lonely planet, for god's sake." She took out her phone and stared at a photo of Yasmina grinning at a track meet, a ribbon around her neck, FIRST PLACE. "What am I gonna do with a travel book?"

"You're old enough to be more independent than you think."

Melody pulled out one of her ear buds. "I'm not one of your college students. You can't just hand me the course syllabus." Her dad reached over and gently patted her arm. Melody shrank away. "You know, I want more than a map and written directions." She stroked her silver bracelet and closed her eyes, tapping her toes as "I Want to Break Free" pulsed in her ears. Her father shook his head.

"Oh, I almost forgot." He leaned over and stuck his hand into his briefcase again. "Aaron stopped by the office to see his mom. He dropped this off for you."

Melody shut off the music and reached for the bulky envelope, turned it over in her hand, and read the scrawled message: TO BE READ ON THE PLANE. As she ripped off the top, a Star of David on a thin silver chain fell into her lap. She pulled out the letter and read it slowly.

Dear Melody,

I hope I am not being too forward, but I want to give this to you for your travels. You are so lucky to have the chance to visit Israel and I want you to stay safe. I know you think I'm nuts, but please wear this Star of David. I have family in Israel, my cousin lives in Kiryat Arba, so I hear about all the stuff that goes on. He's in the military so he knows how dangerous things can be, like in Hebron where Yasmina's family lives. Lots of Arab terrorists there. Most of the country is fine, so just stay out of trouble. Really!!!! I am praying for you. Safe travels.

Your friend,
Aaron

Melody stared at the necklace. She felt teary and annoyed all at once. *Praying for me? Arab terrorists? Really?* She tossed the Star of David up and down a few times. *On the other hand, kinda sweet.* She tilted her head back into the seat and looked up at the overhead panel, stale air blowing into her face. "I know he is a bit of a dork, Mama. But a boy cares about me, that should count for something," she whispered. "Oh, don't be a butt. Whatever am I going to do with this?" She ran her fingers over the star, pulled out her other ear bud and impulsively slipped the chain over her head. "At least I won't lose it, unless of course my head falls off." She smiled at the image, picturing her head, red curls and all, rolling down some ancient stone steps, the Star of David dangling over the edge of a rough gray stair.

Her father didn't notice. He stretched his legs and closed his eyes.

As the cabin became lighter and the slow dawn began, Melody caught a stirring in the plane. She craned her head to peer into the aisles. Clusters of bearded men wrapped in wide prayer shawls, fringes dancing from their white shirts, kippahs perched on their heads, rocked and prayed, noses tucked into their prayer books. Melody poked her dad's arm. He yawned and stared blankly at her. "Dad, what's with the guys in the aisles?"

"Orthodox men, Hassidim, pray at dawn, Mou…I mean honey. You're gonna learn a lot about religion on this trip." She whipped out her phone and surreptitiously snapped a photo. *This is gonna be quite the docudrama.*

"Melody! Don't"

"Research, Dad. Why aren't the women praying? The ones with wigs and scarves, aren't they Orthodox too?"

"Religion. Plus, look at all their kids; they've got their hands full. Now put your phone away."

Just as the flight attendants wheeled the breakfast carts down the aisles, the captain's authoritative voice pierced the quiet clatter. Upcoming turbulence. Melody watched the flurry of activity. Arguments broke out between the attendants and the praying passengers. The ride got bumpier, her stomach lurched. "Please oh please, just stay in the air." She gripped her silver bracelet and closed her eyes tightly.

"All passengers and crew, please return to your seats and fasten your seatbelts IMMEDIATELY." The voice sounded more urgent. Melody's father snatched her hand as tight-lipped attendants raced the carts down the aisles and the plane pitched and heaved, cups and plates clattering wildly. Melody pulled away and bit her lip, rubbing her MOM tattoo. The Star of David bounced across her chest.

Holy crap, the travel goddess is angry. 35,000 feet in the air. Falling out of the sky - definitely a fucking, big risk. Please, please, please. A faint surge of nausea soured in the back of her throat. She grabbed the Star of David and held it tightly in her fist.

After several more big wobbles and lurches, the flight gradually smoothed. A very long fifteen minutes later, the white-knuckled passengers finally loosened their grips. Melody heard a kid vomiting a few rows behind her and several babies screamed incessantly. She inhaled deeply for the first time and smirked. *Maybe the travel goddess is really pissed. I guess all that praying didn't do much good.* She thought for a moment. *Or maybe it did?*

The older woman sitting next to her began chattering with relief. "Well honey, that was a scare. My son made aliyah ten years ago, got real religious, and I'm traveling to my grandson's Bar Mitzvah. God almighty, I want to get there in one piece. They live in Modi'in Illit. Have you heard of it? Lovely new city in Judea and Samaria."

Melody nodded vaguely.

"Dear, do you follow the news? I'm so worried about these Israeli elections. I'm afraid there will be no peace, what with those awful politicians and those Arabs. Do you think there's still hope? I mean, as a member of the younger generation. What do you think?"

Melody shrugged.

"I put my faith in the youth. You know, Israel is such a great start-up nation. My son is in tech, can't really explain what he does, but there is so much promise here. First time, dear?"

Melody nodded.

"You'll love it."

Melody shook her head again and strained to look out the window. The overhead announcements morphed into Hebrew with translations into English. The plane was entering Israeli airspace and passengers were informed they could no longer leave their seats. Melody thought about her full bladder and wished she had planned ahead. She peered across her talkative seatmate. The Mediterranean coast swept into view, high rises started to sprout from the haze and palm trees came into focus. Tel Aviv.

"Mom, we got here," she whispered, her throat tightening. "In one piece. Kinda. Sort of."

Chapter Six

CROSSING THE LINE

MELODY STARED GLUMLY, PEERING THROUGH THE gauzy blue curtains, wedged between her father and a large-bottomed lady. The lady was chattering raucously in Russian with a bleach blond who was sitting in front of her in the white shared minibus. Melody thought about the last few hours, the kerfuffle at the airport, the yelling at the line for this sherut.

She turned toward her father, a bitter feeling at the back of her throat, her tiredness mixing with rage and confusion. "Dad." She held back her tears. "I can't believe you screwed up my birthdate on that form."

"Honey, I was tired, sorry." He stared straight ahead at the highway visible between the blond and a guy with curly black hair and a kippah. Melody's father fidgeted with his fingers, loosely clasped together in his lap.

"But you wrote Mom's birthday instead of mine!" She grabbed his sleeve. "Look at me! Can't you tell the difference?"

He turned slowly to meet her gaze. "Melody, I said I was sorry." She caught his tone, somewhere between scolding and frustration. Condescending.

Melody felt like sorry was not enough. She turned to him, churning inside, and exploded. "Or do you wish I was the one who died?"

"Melody!" The Russian lady and a young couple chattering in Hebrew in the seats behind them stopped and stared. "Enough! Of course not. And I don't appreciate your attitude."

Well, that crossed a line. Melody felt a smug sense of satisfaction. *At least he got it. So not okay. He can't even remember my birthday. Does he see me? ME?* She glowered at her father. *And then the guy at the airport made such a big deal of the mistake. Did he think I was like...some kinda... teenage terrorist? And before that weirdness, all the questioning. Why did Mr. Security need to know my Israeli aunt's name, address and phone number? And was I Jewish? Jewish. That's nobody's business.*

Melody turned to gaze out the window, focusing on the sky, the clouds, escape, her desire to be anywhere but here. *Of course when I said yes, I don't think he believed me. Not too many red headed Sullivans qualify for the chosen people.* She chuckled. The irony of it all. *And then I really flunked when he asked me the name of my rabbi. So stupid. I should have said Aaron. Clearly, "fuck" was not the right answer.*

Melody sighed as the tension in her body sank to its usual midlevel alert status and watched as signs in Hebrew and English flashed by, Ayalon (Canada) National Park, Abu Ghosh, En Neftoah (Lifta). The flat agricultural land got hillier and more houses and apartment buildings flitted past. She looked at her father. He had fallen asleep, but his fist was white, still clenching his briefcase.

Well, he's not the only person who's aggravated. That sherut driver totally lost it when we tried to get into the minibus behind him. I guess he was up next, but what is it with these people? Dad said they were "direct" and "speak their minds, say what they think" and "this can be annoying." Melody nibbled on her fingernail. *The shouting and fist waving. Really? I was just happy that guy didn't have a gun. Or maybe he did, for all I know. Jerko, go directly to anger management therapy. That's what my shrink always says. DIRECTLY.* She shook her head.

Then they had to wait an hour for the minivan Shuttle to Jerusalem to fill. Melody wished she had spoken her mind on that one. But her dad said this was the cheapest way to get to the city and they drop you off at your hotel. *It just cost several years off my life.* She punched her fist into her open palm. *We get dropped off at Damascus Gate and have to walk into the Old City. Walk? I'm so bleary eyed I can barely breathe and swallow at the same time and then he wants me to put one foot in front of the other, dragging my 300 pound suitcase? Shit.* She punched her fist one more time.

As they got closer to the city, loud honking lurched into Melody's consciousness. She held her breath as their sherut swerved around several vehicles. *He's driving like a maniac.* She stared at the whizzing cars inches from the van. *They're all driving like maniacs. Haven't they ever heard of personal space, like in cars?* The sherut pulled off the highway, turned into a residential area, and parked. The young couple behind Melody wriggled out of the van and retrieved their luggage in the back. Melody watched them walk down a stone pathway lined with bursts of orange and yellow canna lilies. Two little children came running out of the apartment, followed by a gray-haired lady, all smiles and kisses. Other kids kicked their heels on a swing in the adjacent playground. *A real family. A normal real family.*

Melody reached into her backpack and pulled out her notebook. She clenched her jaw tightly.

Page four

THE WISH-I-LEFT BEHINDS:

1. *Dad.*
2. *Taking a trip with Dad. Anywhere.*
3. *Turbulence.*
4. *So called airplane food.*
5. *Plastic wrapping. Climate change people!!!!*
6. *Especially plastic knives. Totally useless. And kills whales.*
7. *The smell of toilets on a 10-hour flight.*
8. *Border control agents who think they rule the world.*
9. *People who think you can't be Jewish if you don't have a rabbi.*
10. *Yellers and honkers.*
11. *Cheap ways to get to Jerusalem.*

The sherut pulled back onto the highway. Melody tapped her pen on her notebook. *I guess that's the list. For today.* She put the notebook and pen away and stroked her bracelet, trying to calm down. A snarky "I don't like your attitude" replayed in her brain over and over. *Well, I don't like his attitude either.* She glared at her dad whose head was bobbing backwards, mouth open, deep in sleep. After more stops and turns, the Russian ladies were dropped off at a white stone apartment building and Mr. Curly Hair got out at some sweeping hotel driveway, gray stone, happy faces, couples holding hands. *Looks like everybody's happy here but me.*

The sherut pulled up to its last stop. Melody stared out at the massive plaza, endless steps leading down to a stone gate flanked by towers like the entry to an ancient castle. She shoved her dad's arm. "Dad, wake up." More loudly. "Wake up."

He opened his eyes abruptly, grunted, and sat up straight. "Okay Mouse, okay, okay." He wiped his nose with the back of his hand, shook his head, and slid across the seat. She followed and they both unfolded themselves out of the sherut, stiff from all the sitting. The driver unloaded their suitcases onto a sidewalk bustling with people, chattering in Hebrew, Arabic, and some English and German. A row of Japanese tourists walked by single file, all big sunglasses, smiles, and cameras.

Melody stood uneasily surveying the scene. She pulled her baseball cap over her eyes, squinting from the glaring sun, and heaved her back-pack onto her shoulders. She just wanted to crawl inside of herself and never come out.

Her dad took a very deep breath. He tried to put his hand on her shoulder, but she pulled away. "Look Mel, I need to say something. I know we got off to a rocky start here, but this trip could be really special. Can we do a reset? I'm not perfect, but I need you to understand, I am really trying."

Melody eyed him skeptically. She wanted him to try harder. She looked down at her red sneakers, the left one was untied, and thought about her options. *It's not like I can get back on that plane and fly home. Today. I'm trapped. Like a rat in sneakers.* "Okay, Dad, just don't call me Mouse. Ever." She squatted to tie her shoe.

Her dad nodded, "Okay Ms. Melody Sullivan. That is a deal." She stood up. A look of relief swept across his face. "We gotta head down all these stairs, through that gate, and the hotel is a few blocks into the Old City. I think you'll like it. It's pretty..." he searched for a word, "pretty funky."

"Right, Dad. Funky, that's me." She strained a shadow of a smile.

"And then I'm gonna take you to this neat hole-in-the-wall restaurant that your mom loved. It has great schnitzel wrapped in pita bread. It's a real Israeli dish with hummus and pickles and everything."

"Right Dad, schnitzel." *What the fuck is that? He's just going down memory lane. It's gonna be a long week.*

Chapter Seven

SOLO ADVENTURE

MELODY WOKE ABRUPTLY TO THE DISTANT SOUND of a toilet flushing, the whoosh of rushing water merged with her upsetting dream. She was wildly surfing with her mom, their arms flailing, off balance, curled into a massive wave crashing onto a flat Mediterranean beach. She stretched and shoved her fists against her eyes. "Shit, I don't even know how to surf. Where am I?" She looked around. "God, what time is it?" She wiped some crusted drool from the edge of her lip. "Gross."

The digital clock next to the bed read 11:00 a.m. She stared at the food her father had left: a plate piled with crusted hummus, two boiled eggs, black olives, and two dry pita breads leaning together. "Tomatoes! Doesn't he know I hate them when they're squishy? Ugh. And that hummus stuff looks like vomit."

She pulled the sheets over her head and thought about yesterday, a blur of churches, white stone, falafel sandwiches, people yapping in anything but English. Her father pontificating happily about this relic and that famous whatever. He was talking so loudly. So embarrassing. *Then he leaves me here, the whole day, while he's at that stupid conference.*

The solitude of the quiet bedroom, the humming of the fan overhead, the heavy yellowed curtains, all sucked the air out of the room, making it hard to breathe. Melody felt like she was choking; small, totally alone, invisible in a strange bed, strange hotel, strange city. A wave of fear and loneliness swept over her. She bit her lip, dragging her teeth against the soft redness. *I could just die here and who would know?* She imagined her father coming back in the evening, finding her cold body tangled in the blanket.

Fuck this.

She sat up, flung the sheets off, inhaled a deliberate deep breath through her nose and let the air blow gently out of her pursed lips. She reached for her father's note.

Morning, sweetie. Had to leave early for the conference. Hope you had a good sleep before day one of your big solo adventure.

Solo adventure? Sounds like Amelia Earhart or something. Dad, remember she was lost at sea, like when her plane crashed?

Check out the Lonely Planet. I've highlighted some good spots for you. Hope you have a super day. Don't forget to eat. And drink lots of water. BOTTLED WATER!!! Dinner at 7. Shekels on the dresser. Meet here.

Aaron's note lay beside her father's.

She slid back into the bedding, holding Aaron's letter in one hand and a hard-boiled egg in the other. "I could just sleep all day," she said out loud and yawned noisily. "Wish I had some salt for these eggs. God, this time change...brutal." She read Aaron's note again. *Safe travels. Your friend, Aaron.* She touched the Star of David draped around her neck, resting on her black tee shirt. *What kind of friend is he, really? He cares about me...which is so, so sweet. Not sure if I care about him, really. He's such a dork. Maybe he could be just a friend, a good friend. Whatever that is. Well, Ms. Manners, the least you can do is thank him for the necklace.*

She reached for her phone which was leaning against a lamp as if it too needed support. The phone was plugged into an adaptor which was plugged into the wall. *Even the electricity around here is foreign.* She tapped the phone, cradling it in her palm like a dear friend, thumbs ready to rap.

Dear Aaron, thank you for... *No, too formal.* Melody shook her head and frowned.

Hey Aaron, guess where I am? *Mel, he knows where you are. Don't be stupid.*

What do I want to say? I need some air in here, clear my head. Melody wiggled out of bed, pulled the heavy drapes apart, and slid the window open a crack as dense warm air drifted against her hand. Arabic calls to prayer resonated through her room, deep sonorous voices echoing from mysterious places outside her window. Somewhere, church bells bonged in a strange symphonic cacophony.

She stared at the view, a jumble of gray-and-cream colored, flat-roofed houses, rooftop laundry strung out to dry in the sultry sun. Her eyes swept over giant crosses stretching skyward, black water tanks baking, skinny minarets pointing at the scattered clouds, and a shimmery golden dome ringed by dark, pointy evergreens in the background.

Hello, Jerusalem. Wow. She leaned against the window and just looked, her nose squashed to the glass. Her pulse slowed. The calm beauty of it all. She reached for her phone.

Hey Aaron, I wish you could see what I'm seeing.

Idiot, take a picture. Remember, docudrama? She ran her fingers through her tangled hair and posed for a selfie, pouting, the cityscape in the background. She tried a thumbs up, her face half in, half out of the shot with the golden dome lighting up the outline of her curls. Click. Click. Click. She held up the necklace and grinned. Click.

Hey Aaron, this is the view from my window. I thought you would like it. Never thought I'd be wearing a Star of David, but here I am. Thanks...She stopped and wrinkled her nose. *Thanks for thinking of me. Hope Cheddar is OK. Give him a puppy hug for me.* She tapped send. *That's done.*

Melody sat down on the edge of the bed and bit into the egg. The dense yellow yolk crumpled and fell onto Aaron's letter, obliterating *safe travels,* then bounced into the folds of her pillow. Her phone pinged.

You're wearing it? Totally cool.

Melody rolled her eyes. *Don't get too excited,* she tapped. She stopped. *Don't be a jerk. The guys being nice.* Delete.

Actually, totally hot here. ☺, 😆, 🔥 She laughed. *I'll keep you posted.*

Really happy to hear that. Stay chill. Cheddar's great. 👋, ☼, 🛏, 🐶

Gotta get up - start my day, or at least my afternoon. See you. 👋

Melody glanced at the splattered fragments of egg. *Klutzo.* She picked the yolk off the pillow and popped the bits in her mouth. *Get up. Ooo, I have to pee. Really bad. Where'd they put the toilet?*

As she brushed her teeth, she stared into the mirror in the surfboard-size bathroom, her eyes smudged with yesterday's mascara, her red curls gone totally berserk, the minty smell of toothpaste and lemony soap filling the air. The Star of David hung askew over her shoulder. She splashed soap on her cheeks, scrubbed vigorously, and skeptically looked at her face, picking at her chin.

Melody spotted a blotch near her left nostril. *Pimple?* She stretched her upper lip over her teeth and looked more closely. Freckle. She sighed, acknowledging her daily ritual, her daily wave of disappointment. *Why didn't I get my mom's skin? Fightin' Irish sperm, as Daddy says. My luck.* She grimaced at the mirror, checking her teeth. *No egg stuck on those chompers.*

As she moved out of the bathroom, she grabbed her baseball cap, squashed her unruly curls down, and climbed back into bed. Her doggy pajama bottoms rumpled up toward her knees as she stretched out her legs. She flipped the travel book open. Her dad had stuck sticky notes on the pages in the section on Jerusalem, and highlighted the parts he considered important in yellow, with comments in red on the margins. *Does he think this book is a stupid term paper?* She gazed at a map of the Old City, crisscrossed with corkscrew streets with strange-sounding names and bolded numbers denoting something Very Important and Old.

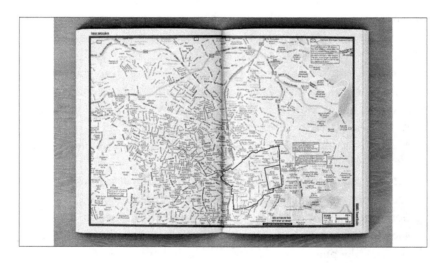

She peeled off two stickies scrawled with messages from her father and stuck them to her thumbs.

> *Sticky #1 Your mom and I loved this city, Here's where your mom and I met, at the Austrian hospice, when we were grad students, (we fell in love to the sounds and smells of Jerusalem). She always wanted to come back.*

Dad, TMI. T-M-I. Just the thought of her mom and dad kissing under some palm tree was more than Melody could tolerate.

Sticky #2 Hope you can feel the history and the splendor of the ancient architecture. Just keep your eyes open and take it all in. I am so in love with this city. Wish you could be too.

Wish he paid as much attention to me as he does to this frigging pile of stones. Melody turned to the highlighted page.

Jerusalem's Old City... Wide-eyed with awe, pilgrims flood into the walled city to worship at locations linked to the very foundation of their faith. Church bells, Islamic calls to prayer and the shofar (Jewish ram's horn) electrify the air with a beguiling, if not harmonious, melody.

Red arrow: *Mel, look and listen for churches, synagogues, and mosques. Be sure to read about the history - see pp. 47-51.*

Melody rolled her eyes and peeled off another yellow note.

Sticky #3 Be sure to see the Western Wall - go into the underground museum, thousands of years of amazing history as you wind down the stairs going deeper into antiquity. Your mom loved that place. For an atheist, she said this was where she had her finest spiritual moments.

Melody suddenly felt tears rising. At home, the memory of her mom haunted her. The photos on the wall, the bedspread they picked out together, the tart rhubarb pie she taught her to bake. The scars on her wrist. And now her mom was here, lurking in every corner. *God, she even haunts Dad.*

Red arrow. *Good paragraph on Mamluk architecture p.69.*

I can't deal with him. Makes me want to stick my finger down my throat. Mamluk? Really?

She flopped back on the bed. *What am I gonna do?* She stared up at the ceiling and noticed the fan swinging slowly around and around, like it was lost in thought. She stretched over her bed and grabbed her pack, pulled out her notebook. *Where's that pen?* The point on the page made a comforting, scratching sound, the black ink curling into each letter, holding her softly.

Page five

While warm air wraps my face,
A fan swings slowly over my head,
I wish I could just close my eyes,
I lie unhappily in this bed.
My hope is gone, my sorrow deep,
I do not know what lies ahead.

Melody scratched her red curls and took a breath, enveloped in her loneliness.

My life spins like that humming fan,
My heart is filled with tears and dread,
Each day is gray and endless now,
Am I alive or possibly dead?

"That sucks. Bring out the violins." Melody folded the notebook closed and dabbed her moist eyes with the edge of the sheet. *Drama, drama.* She shoved the book under her pillow and sighed.

"Daddy thinks I'm gonna wander all over this place, admiring an-ti-qui-ty." She bounced each syllable off her tongue. "While he goes to his ridiculous conference. That is so not happening. But I've got to do something. There's always sleeping…or shopping." Melody bent her elbow, rested her chin on her closed fist, and mulled over her options. *I could get Aaron his baby camel. Or whatever. What would he want?*

She sat up straight, the idea spinning in her head. *I'm so afraid of getting totally L-O-S-T. I could just stay in this room.* She looked around. *No TV. Where did Dad say this hotel was?* She turned to the side table and spotted a pad of paper. He had circled in red ink: Hashimi Guesthouse, Suq Khan El Zeit St. no 85 Old City. "I should take you with me so I've got a fighting chance of getting back here," she announced to the stationary.

She picked up the guide book and stared, thumbing through "Old City, Top Sights." "Gotta be something about shopping. There's Christian Quarter. Lots of sticky notes. Nooo. Armenian Quarter, whatever that is. Muslim Quarter, definitely not Aaron. Jewish Quarter. Yes." She threw up her fist in a sign of victory.

Melody opened to her dad's sticky on p. 65, Jewish Quarter, Western Wall. Yellow highlighter screamed at her.

Judaism's holiest prayer site, where worshippers recite scriptures, lay their hands on 2000-years-old stone and utter impassioned prayers.

She stared at the red arrow.

Like I said, a must, for your mom. AND FOR YOU. This would make her so happy.

Melody crumpled sticky note #3 and threw it across the bed. *She's dead, Dad. Beyond happy. Totally dead.*

The area immediately in front of the wall now operates as a great open-air synagogue, exerting a pull discernable even to nonreligious visitors.

Her father had underlined nonreligious twice.

It's divided into two areas: a small southern section for women and a much larger northern section for men...

Oh that's really great. Sexist shit. Even here.

She flipped the page and scanned.

Red arrow: *stones from Herod the Great reign 37 - 4 BCE*

Red arrow: *Al Aqsa Mosque 600s AD*

Melody stared up at the languid fan, "Dad, could you please control yourself? Oh-oh, I'm talking to myself, so not a good sign." She smirked, shook her curls, and finished off the other egg.

Melody stood up, grabbed an olive, and paced toward the curtained window, reading the guide and waving the olive like a magic wand.

...visible at close quarters are the wads of paper stuffed into cracks between the stones.

She grabbed the crumpled sticky note from the bed. "And here is exhibit A." She pushed it into the wall. It dropped to the floor.

> *Some Jews believe that prayers and petitions inserted between the stones have a better-than-average chance of being answered... Prayers are also accepted in digital form...on the Kotel website...*

www.g-o-d.org. I'm such a heathen. She looked at the crumpled note on the floor. *I guess he's not listening. Or she.* She smirked. *Or they. Or whatever.* She slumped on the bed. Her eyes fell on another highlighted page:

> *At one time the Cardo would have run the whole breadth of the city...but in its present form it starts just south of David St, the tourist souq, serving as the main entry into the Jewish Quarter from the Muslim and Christian areas.*

Melody turned the book sideways and squinted.

> *You like to shop?* Scrawled in red. *A souq is a market. Check it out.*

Chapter Eight

LOST AND FOUND

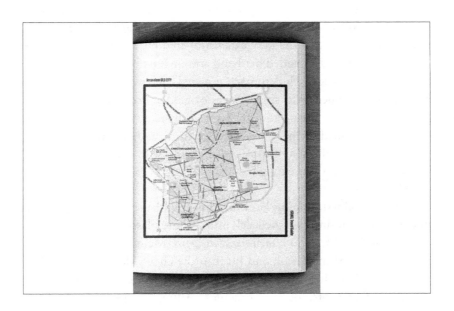

'M SO *L-O-S-T. I CAN'T EVEN SAY THE WORD.* Melody gazed up at the winding stone street, the graceful archways, the narrow stairways meandering off on either side, and stared at the creased map tucked into the back of the *Lonely Planet.* She could hear her father's voice. "Study the map Mouse. You could just drive off a cliff if you listened to that google lady. Use your brains, look around."

Why did he think I could do this? It's not like I'm Ms. World Traveler or anything. These streets are so...so...convoluted. Vermont cow paths are straighter than this. Melody bit her lip and sucked in her rising tears. Her face flushed, her freckles deepening. *God, no blubbering now. Not here. Not alone. How am I gonna find the fucking camel? Or fucking breakfast for that matter.*

She looked around. It didn't help. She reached for her phone, tapped on her downloaded google map, searched Cardo, Jerusalem. Not much help either. She rotated the screen, trying to figure out which way was which. *It's a maze. Didn't these guys wander in the desert for 40 years? What did I expect? This place is old. Like really, really old. Like no TV, smartphone, flush toilets old.*

She nervously stopped in front of a crowded souvenir shop, a wall of kitschy postcards, rows of brightly patterned scarfs, and cheap plastic toys and trucks from China, embroidered caps and small figurines carved from olive wood. *No baby camels here. Lots of baby Jesuses. Not That Helpful.* Two scrawny gray cats scampered by, looking hungry. She crouched down and extended her hand and then had second thoughts. "I feel your pain kitties." Her stomach growled. She stood up and spotted a table outside piled with small loaves of golden crusted breads, round pizzas topped with cheese and some greenish spice, and…weird oblong bagels? She smiled at the young man behind the table, pointed at the elongated bagel things, and took ten shekels out of the front pocket of her jeans, hoping it was enough.

"One ka'ek?"

Melody nodded, hoping ka'ek meant weird bagel. He handed her a pile of coins and dropped the ka'ek into a white plastic bag.

"Thanks." *Ka'ek, gotta remember that word.* Melody hungrily opened the bag, grabbed the bread, and bit into the chewy dough. The sesame seeds danced on her tongue. She stopped in front of another shop, mounds of apricots, dates, pistachios, walnuts, almonds. Her eyes widened. *Score.*

What did Dad say? A shekel is kinda like a quarter? She slid her backpack off and squatted on the edge of a stair, her knees popping out of the holes in her jeans like two eyeballs watching the street. In the bag where she kept her passport she felt a fold of bills. She took out twenty shekels, stood up, pointed at the apricots and the pistachios, and handed the shopkeeper the money.

Melody's mood lifted as a surge of energy skittered through her body. She crunched on a pistachio, enjoying the salty sweet nuttiness. As she turned quickly away she knocked against a teenage girl in a long blue skirt and loose blouse. "Sorry."

"It's okay. No harm done. I see you like apricots."

A human who speaks real English. Thank you, lord. "Yes, and I like pistachios too."

The young woman laughed and adjusted her glasses. "Visiting from the States?"

"How can you tell? Do I look that lost?" Melody liked her smile. "I'm Melody, Melody Sullivan."

Melody stared at the thick long braid cascading from under her gray scarf, the baggy sleeves wrapped snugly around her wrists. *Muslim? Jewish? Maybe a nun? Who the hell knows around here?*

"Sarah Levy. Welcome to Jerusalem."

Melody spotted a Star of David hanging around the young woman's neck. "Could you help me? I'm trying to get to the Jewish Quarter, the Cardo to be exact. Need to get a present for a friend."

"Sure, that's simple." Sarah pointed to a street.

"Simple for you." Melody grinned.

"I live in the Jewish Quarter."

"Really? I didn't know people actually live here. I mean, I know that sounds stupid, but, people actually live here? Do you want a bite?" Melody ripped off a piece of the half-eaten ka'ek.

Sarah laughed. "No thanks. You do need help. Follow me."

Melody rocked back and forth on her red sneakers, relieved, hopeful. The tension in her body headed south. "Your English sounds so…American."

"My grandparents were born in the States, Cleveland. They made aliya in '67, after the war." Sarah nodded. "So my ima, I mean my mom, grew up speaking English. But she was born in Jerusalem."

"Oh." Melody wondered. *What war was that?* "What's a-li-ya?'"

"Moving to Israel, it's like making a spiritual journey. It means we came home, as G-d promised."

"Ohhh." *A weird god freak. What did I expect, it's Jerusalem.* "Your dad?"

"My aba was born here too, but his family came years earlier. From Europe. You know, Holocaust survivors."

"Right." Melody wasn't sure what to say. At least she'd heard of the Holocaust. "I read *The Diary of Anne Frank*. I'm sorry."

Sarah nodded again. "That's why we need to be here." She tipped her head sympathetically and headed into the crowds, weaving through winding streets bustling with local shoppers and tourists. Melody fixed her gaze on Sarah's long braid; she wished she could hold on to it. As Melody trailed behind her, she heard a babble of Hebrew, Arabic, some Japanese, German, maybe some French. Shopkeepers captured her eye as they gestured toward their stores piled with embroidery, pictures of

Al Aqsa Mosque, cheap suitcases, a rainbow of embroidered dresses and scarves hanging above their heads. "Lady, for you, special bargain for you. Young lady with beautiful red hair…" *Don't look around. Follow the braid.*

Traipsing up and down stone stairs and streets, through crowded bazaars, the wafting smells of cardamom and strong coffee, Melody felt like she was on a quest, maybe the stage set for a movie, maybe in some weird ancient kingdom with a lot of extras hoping for parts. She fully expected a crusader in full body armor or maybe some bearded white guy in a toga to come sauntering along holding a stone tablet. Finally, they came to a narrow passageway that led into the Jewish Quarter.

"You okay?"

Melody smiled and held both hands out in a shrug. *That's an existential question.*

"Have fun." Sarah waved. "This is the Cardo." She pointed at the rows of high-end shops and sparkling displays. "Hope you find what you are looking for. Some of the stuff is real expensive, so watch the prices. Yalla, bye."

Melody waved back. "Yalla. Bye. Thank you." As Sarah disappeared, she yelled, "You saved me." *Jesus, I should have left breadcrumbs, actually ka'ek crumbs. Will I ever find my hotel?* She looked up at the cavernous arches of the shopping arcade, the shops set deeply into old vaults, the arched roof built to let in a glowing natural light. *It's like a totally different world in here. Like some kind of weird biblical mall.* The golden white stones were spotless. Blue and white Israeli flags drooped at doorways. She walked past a display of shoes, piles of colorful knitted kippahs, prayer shawls hanging in multi-layered rows. She wandered into a shop with a colorful Judaica sign. *Sounds like Mezuzah Land to me. And here they are.* Melody smiled and clapped. *Dah dah. Victory. Forget the camels.*

Melody felt a sudden urge to text Aaron. She snapped a selfie with the store behind her, finger pointing at the displays, making a cutie face, lips puckered, then aimed her phone at the knitted skullcaps. Click, click.

Hey Aaron, what do you think? What's your price range?

Ur actually looking? 😜

Don't be a dork. Yes I'm looking. Kippa, mazuza, spelling??? 🙈

Ur sweet. 🤍, 👏

Actually lonely, except I met a Jewish angel - in charge of directions. 😥

Really?? HAHAHA.

No really. Which one?

Which angel???

Stupid, which kippa? mazuza?

You pick. Ceramic ones are nice. ☞

Melody picked up a blue and white mezuzah with Hebrew lettering. Click. *This one?*

Nice, how much?

She looked at the tag. *110.*

Dollars???? 🙀

Dummy, I'm in Israel, shekels. Like $25. 💵

Sure, that one. ☺

Got it.

The guy's real easy to please. What's with him? Melody headed to the cashier.

Her phone pinged.

Take me with you.

What???? 😦

Ur in Jerusalem. So jealous. Show me. Let's go to the Western Wall.

Really?

Really? Let's go together. Just me and you. Virtual. 🙏

Melody hesitated. *A date? What the hell is he saying?* She sighed. *Well, it's not like anyone else is offering.* She stared at the phone for a while and a pressure rose in her throat.

The sales lady behind the counter leaned forward, impatiently. "Well…can I help you?" Her voice grew strident. "Or are you going to take all day?"

Melody looked up at her, surprised. She cradled her phone. Her thumbs flew. *First let me try to get out of here. Attack by monster sales lady.* ☺, 👹 👺

Melody dug into her backpack for shekels. "Sorry I'm taking so long. Is this enough?"

Chapter Nine

GUIDED TOUR

MELODY TRAILED BEHIND A GUIDE HOLDING a bright orange flag followed by a cluster of tourists with crosses and Bibles in hand, snapping photos and chattering in a slow drawl. *Texas? Mega-church Jesus freaks? Who walks around clutching Bibles?*

"The Cardo was comprised of a central lane, open to the sky, for the passage of carriages and animals, flanked on each side by colonnaded covered walkways for pedestrians. As we walk through the domed Cardo," the guide stopped and pointed, "we come to a place where we can look down through this Plexiglass window and see two ancient city walls...." Everyone craned their heads and took photos. "The wall of Hezekian from the eighth century BCE and the Hasmoniean wall from the second century BCE..." Melody peeked too.

Her mind flip flopped. *BCE? That stands for?* She looked around at the clutch of mesmerized believers. *Ahh. Before Christ. Way before flush toilets.*

The tourists strolled into a big room, and the guide held up his flag and stopped. Melody dawdled at the back. "See this mosaic map on the wall, the Madaba. It's a replica of a larger map in the floor of a church in Madaba, Jordan. Dates to the sixth century." The group formed a half circle around the mosaic and started snapping more photos. "This portion of the map shows Jerusalem with the Cardo going all the way to the Holy Sepulcher and the NEA Church of Mary. Can anyone see what is missing?" The tourists stared blankly. "Folks, you will notice the Jewish Temple Mount is not here." Melody heard a low rumble of dear gods and what do you knows.

"As we arrive toward the end of the Cardo, you can see this beautiful painting of what the shopping area looked like during the Roman/Byzantine period." The group circled around again. "You are standing on the original Byzantine stones, left behind after the destruction of the city." Melody watched the tourists shifting their feet and staring at the floor. "During the excavation after the Six Day War in 1967, archeologists found that under the modern buildings are the remains of the rest of the Cardo."

1967 That date again. 1967 - Six Day War. Melody crunched her eyebrows together and looked at the guide. *He would know. But I should shut up.*

"Then we are going to take the stairway up and out of the Cardo and we will reach the modern Jewish Quarter."

Up and out sounds like my plan.

"But before we get to the open plaza, you will see a large ditch with a twenty-one-foot thick rock wall, a portion of the wall built by Hezekiah in the late eighth century BCE. Excuse me miss, can we help you?"

Melody blushed. "No thanks. Sorry." She wended her way around the Texans and fled up the stairs.

Chapter Ten

WE'RE ALL HERE

MELODY SHIELDED HER EYES AS SHE EMERGED onto the street.
Still there?
Damn. Aaron. *Got tangled up...Texas Jesus freaks.*

🙁

Gotta check my directions.

Melody leaned against the stone wall and opened her map. *Jewish Quarter.* Her eyes darted around the crisscross of streets on the map. *Here's the Western Wall.*

I'm an inch away. Give me five minutes.

Where's my angel when I need her? She turned toward an older woman wearing a loose scarf around her hair. "'Scuse me. English? Western Wall?" The woman pointed toward a sign, Misgav Ladach Street.

"Take a right on Ma'alot Rabi Yehuda HaLevi, take stairs through a covered tunnel. You can't miss it, dear." *Thick Hebrew accent.*

Melody nodded, bewildered. She leaned against the stone wall. *Ma-ah what? Shit.* She sank down onto the stone street, pretzeled against the wall. *Deep breath.* Melody watched the parade of legs and feet, sandals, sneakers, clip clopping heels, the swish of a long dress, her eyes at knee level. *Okay Mom, I can do this. For you.* She twirled her bracelet around her wrist a few times and kissed the braided silver and then the emeralds. They felt cool and calming on her lips.

She stood up and adjusted her baseball cap. *Just look for a street that starts with M. Thank god the signs are in English too. It's only a map inch. How far could that be?* A soccer ball bounced against her leg as a group of young boys wearing knitted kippahs, fringes dancing from under their shirts, yelled, "Slicha, gveret."

Melody glared at them, then shrugged and rolled her eyes. She followed the stone steps that morphed back and forth onto a road, in and out of the shade of arched walkways. A vague sense of panic started to build. She could feel her pulse speeding up, a pounding in her chest. *I know what to do. Inhale. Like the shrink always says. Now exhale. Slowly. At least Aaron knows where I am, I mean where I am trying to be.* A cluster of yeshiva students in black coats and tall black hats hurried past, followed by a young woman carrying a toddler. "Western Wall?" The young lady pointed to the right and soon Melody emerged onto a large open plaza teaming with people.

She stopped. Her gaze swept across the impressive space, the swarms of tourists, the clusters of men. She did a double take when two fully bearded men in tall fur hats and long black coats hustled by, carefully avoiding her, long tight curls bouncing on each side of their faces. They were chatting intently. *Are those the true believers? Why the curls? Gotta research dress codes around here. Don't they know it's summer?*

She stopped and stared at them carefully, her mind racing. *What century are they living in?* She thought for a moment. An older teen in a long skirt and tight kerchief walked by, pushing a wide baby carriage, twins. *Christ. What's it like to be a teenage mother around here? Married? Pregnant? Damn.* Melody shook her head. *Whatever happened to population control and girl power and the twenty-first century?* She watched the tall hats and kerchief disappear into the crowds. *Got lost in the desert?*

She recognized two Bar Mitzvahs, like her friends back home, but way different. Two boys rocked back and forth, reading their Torah portions, surrounded by men draped in long prayer shawls. The giant wall loomed in the background like a poster for The Holy City. Israeli flags hung everywhere, slouching in the still air, and soldiers loitered aimlessly. Mothers sat on white plastic chairs, shaded under white umbrellas, swaying baby carriages back and forth. Babies cried. A pigeon swooped close to her face. Beyond the teaming crowds loomed the ancient cream-colored wall, the golden dome above gleaming like a sunrise, topped by deep blue sky and the occasional cotton-ball cloud.

Melody took a deep breath. *So this is how people get religion.* She took her phone from her back pocket and snapped a few photos, including a selfie with eyes and mouth wide open, and a video sweeping across the entire scene.

Aaron, I'm here. She pulled her baseball hat forward to shield her eyes. *I mean we're here.* She tapped send.

WOW!!! BIG WOW!!! SO AWESOME!!

Melody smirked a half-smile. She hated to admit how awed she felt. It was pretty impressive.

THANK YOU!!! ♡, 😊, 🙏

Get a grip, Aaron.

Really, this means a lot. Always dreamed of having my Bar Mitzvah here.

Why??? Melody rolled her eyes.

It's such a sacred space. *** MOST IMPORTANT RELIGIOUS SITE FOR JEWS EVER***.

Why?

Ever heard of the Second Temple?

Not exactly. 😕

Year 70. Romans destroyed the Jewish temple. This wall is all that remains. REALLY IMPORTANT.

Got it. Mr. Rabbi Historian.

And you are sharing this moment with ME!!! 😮

😵

We liberated Jerusalem in '67. Now EVERYONE can pray here. It's SO GREAT.

We???? Not born yet.

We the Jewish People. Our homeland. Promised in the Bible. A MODERN MIRACLE. ⚡, 🙏

Don't believe in miracles. Melody frowned and shook her head, unsettled and agitated by Aaron's enthusiasm. Where does he get this stuff? She felt this strange connection with him and, at the same time, an ocean of distance. The physical space in the plaza was so vast, yet so weird. And Aaron was so…transfixed. She studied the clusters of people; everyone seemed lost in their own little universe. *What did this place feel like for my mom? Who was she then? What was her universe?*

She started walking toward the wall, trying to imagine her mom, her sandaled feet on these same stones, feeling the heat of the same sun, falling in love with her dad who was young and adventurous (and not an awful human being yet). His flaming red hair standing out in a crowd. *Did they hold hands? Laugh? Kiss? Ugh. Then. Here.* She took an intense deep breath and a heavy weight sank in her body. She knew how that story ended.

You still there?

Melody paused. *Thinking about my mom, she loved this place.*

Must be tough. 😕*Take your time. I can wait.*

Suddenly, she felt like Aaron could see inside of her, like a melon cracked open with a million tender seeds. *Take your time.* Melody stopped and stared at the phone, cupping it tightly with both hands, like some kind of life raft. *You're right. More than tough.*

Melody kept walking, her hard edges softening with Aaron's attention. *Walls up? Walls down? Too. Much. Vulnerable.* She spotted the white barriers separating the men from the women near the wall. *Damn, that so pisses me off.* Her gloom and helplessness melted into irritation.

I wish I could be there with you.

You kinda are.

Kinda.

Did you know that men and women have to pray separately???? SO UNFAIR!!!

Ancient traditions.

Like foot binding??? 😖 , 👣

It's a holy place!!! 🛐

Ancient sexism Aaron.

My rabbi said women are more spiritual so they don't need to pray.

HAHA! Not this woman. 😼

I don't believe him. It will change, you'll see.

Doubt it. Melody felt awash with a heave of emotion. Her anger clashing with her genuine amazement, her deep sense of loss contained by Aaron's concern. Her memories of her mom. Her sort of date with Aaron. *So bizarro.*

Do me a favor?

What?

I want to leave a prayer at the wall. 🙏

No paper. Melody stared at her phone. Silence. Her heart sank. Two teenage girls walked around her, chattering in Hebrew. A couple held hands as they strolled by, the bearded man gesturing at the wall and the entrance to the tunnel museum. Melody thought about her mom and dad. *Did they touch here? Look longingly at each other here? Kiss?* She startled when the phone pinged.

I'll text it.

Don't be stupid.

Really, just don't look.

Melody gazed up at the ocean of sky and shook her head. *This place makes people crazy. But the guy's serious about this.* She sighed.

Okay Bar Mitzvah boy.

She walked into the partitioned section and wended her way between women chatting, praying, crying, touching the ancient stones, rocking back and forth. The phone pinged.

U hold the phone against the wall, and DON'T LOOK!!!

Melody groaned. *OK.*

She wiggled between two older women engrossed in prayer and stared closely at the wall. Between the large chiseled square stones, patches of green shrubby plants erupted as if in religious ecstasy. She spotted tiny lizards darting skyward and a dove's nest nestled in a crack high above her head. White flowers with delicate purple stamens bloomed stubbornly. The cracks between the stones were stuffed with folded bits of paper. Her phone pinged. She looked around, self-consciously, leaned forward, and held the phone against one of the cracks, sliding the edge between the stones, shielding it with her hand. She counted to ten.

The phone pinged again. *THANK YOU. REALLY REALLY MEANINGFUL FOR ME. DON'T LOOK.* 🙏 , 🙂, 👏

Melody backed away and sat down on a plastic chair. The sun and thick air weighted her down as if her body would soon flatten into a melted blob dripping onto the stones. Sweat gathered under her hat. She swallowed, slightly guilty, scrolled up to the earlier text, and read.

Sh'ma Yisra'el, Adonai eloheinu, Adonai 'ehad. Hashem. Let me be a learned and wise rabbi and kind and smart. Let me help my friend Melody find her way out of her sadness. She has a beautiful soul. I want to be close to her. I think I love her. Amen. Aaron Shapiro, Vermont, USA.

Shit. He's serious. A rivulet of tears dribbled across her freckles and trickled down her chin, dripping onto her phone. She felt herself exploding and shattering, melon seeds everywhere. Melody leaned back on her plastic chair, remembering his dimples, long lanky legs, unruly hair, the long curve of the back of his neck. *Like a gazelle.* She seriously wanted to hug him. She shoved the phone into her pocket, curled her body around her folded arms, and rocked back and forth, holding herself tight, quietly weeping.

Weeping about everything.

Chapter Eleven

FIRST KISS

MELODY CATAPULTED UP THE STAIRS INTO THE LOBBY of the guest-house, nodded at the clerk standing behind the marble check-in desk, and bolted past the red, heavily upholstered chairs and up the next flight to her room. As she opened the door, the air felt hot and suffocating. She flipped on the fan, flopped on the bed, and reached for her pack, pulling out her notebook.

What is that expression? But for the kindness of strangers? I'd be L-O-S-T forever. At least I actually made it back here. How many wrong turns can one person make in a day? In this city? In a life? God, it's stuffy in here. She sat up abruptly and grabbed her room key, pack, and notebook.

Melody headed up another flight and opened a door onto the roof deck, surveying the half-circles of wicker chairs, potted red geraniums, and graceful palm trees arching under a thatched roof. She put her note-book, phone, and backpack down on a wicker side table after moving an ashtray full of crumpled cigarette butts (*gross!*) and walked over to a small fridge. She grabbed a Coke, the cool glass sweating in the warm air, and arranged herself in a chair, her body completely in the shade. She rubbed her forehead with the icy bottle, pulled down her cap, and chewed on a ringlet of red hair that had escaped her curly-hair-out-of-control manage-ment program. She closed her eyes.

Aaron floated into her thoughts, like he was riding one of those clouds she saw from the plane window. Waving. *Must be nighttime back home. Aaron. In his PJs. Sprawled on his bed. Did he take his kippah off at night? Was he staring at her selfies?*

She felt an urgent need to hear Yaz's voice, girl-talk about the day, the Aaron developments.

She grabbed her phone.

Yaz, you there? 😋, 🙂

Can't talk now. Sorry. 😯

Why????

In the bosom of my family. Lots to tell you.
Got a fiancé yet??????
NO NO NO. Developments on the home front. Gotta go.
I got lots to tell you too.
Sorry.

What's with her? I thought she was my BFF, my sister sister. Well, I hope she likes the scarf I got her. Melody slurped her drink, relieved by the sweet taste of cold on her tongue. Cleansing. She pulled the scarf out of her pack, the silver threads sparkling, woven into soft greens and blues. *It will make a great hijab. Her deep brown eyes. Golden skin. Definitely her colors.* She laughed, thinking about her clumsy attempts to bargain with the shopkeeper. Sign language, pointing at shekels, trying to look disinterested. *I'm sure I paid the white American tourist price. Shit, that's what I am. The Arab quarter was like so third-world exotic. And then I noticed the scarf was made in Bangladesh. Go figure. At least I bought it in the Old City. That should mean something.*

Melody stretched out her legs. She felt exhausted. Aaron kept popping into her thoughts. Shy, dreamy, klutzy, nervous Aaron. She could see his long pale fingers enveloping his phone, his thumbs hitting each letter. B-E-A-U-T-I-F-U-L-space-S-O-U-L. She felt an urge to hold his hand, to touch his face. His dimples looked, she searched for a word, they looked adorable. *I really need his photo. Really really. Smiling. In my phone. Could I ask him for a selfie? Not a cross-eyed goofy shot, but just his face staring at me…across the Atlantic. With that serious, yearning look. God, I'm turning into mush.*

She looked up at the expanse of blue sky and tried breathing slowly. *Oh dear, I'm becoming one with the universe. Help me. Help me.* She chuckled, shook her head, and reached for her notebook.

Page six

Dear Mom,
Melody tried to remember the last time her mom saw Aaron. End of elementary school? A university party, maybe trailing along after his mom who was drinking a glass of white wine, chattering? Melody's father serving, as usual? Aaron quiet, as usual. He was definitely little. Before even a glimmer of facial hair. Her brain jumped to that time Aaron's legs bonked into hers at The Buttered Biscuit, the shiver that shook her body,

like a freaky shock. An electrical connection. *He definitely has facial hair now.*

> *Mom, I think it's really happening. His name is Aaron. He's cute, hair like a Muppet, kinda shy. Studious. Sincere. Caring. You knew him from preschool. Was he the thumb-sucker kid? But he's changed. Obviously. Much taller. Bigger thumbs. HAHAHA.*
>
> *Seriously. I can't stop thinking about him. Really too religious. Does that matter? I guess we sorta balance each other out in the god department.*
>
> *He stays up late, waiting for my messages. He says I have a *beautiful soul.* Actually not directly to me, but I did something sort of bad. I read his <u>private</u> text. To god. See what I mean?*
>
> *I don't think that really counts as bad if there is no god. What do you think? I never asked you what you thought about her existence. What DO you think?*
>
> *So I have another bad thought. I think it is really bad!!! Traveling with Dad, I feel like my wrong parent died. I know that is awful, but now I have said it. I really don't wish Dad was actually dead, dead, dead, but that is how I feel. I miss you so much. Are you angry with me now? LONELY SAD. CRY CRY CRY.*
>
> *Back to Mr. Rabbi, that's what I call Aaron. We went on a first date!!! Virtual. Is that what you meant by safe sex? Just joking. HAHA. Don't worry, never been kissed. Maybe I should worry? Big sigh. I think I should worry. I'm pretty old for firsts. I wish you could tell me what kissing really feels like, I mean not like kissing grandma, but really kissing.*

Melody put her notebook down in her lap as the sun splashed at her toes. She wondered if the sun really had enormous glowing eyeballs that saw everything, like a giant video camera. Did it remember her mom and dad, or her and Aaron? *OMG, am I getting all celestial and weird? Maybe sunstroke?* She puckered her lips together, pressed them on the back of her hand, and made a slow smacking sound. Like a kiss. Like a first kiss. She wondered if Aaron's lips would feel soft and alive, all quivery and nervous. Not like in the movies where everyone knew what they were doing.

> *You had your first date with Dad here, in the Old City, right? Can't imagine you really kissing Dad. Yuck.* ☹
>
> *Aaron thinks I'm funny, and he worries about me. No one actually worries about me now that you are gone. Except Yaz. Dad is his usual MIA.*
>
> *Aaron is dorky, but he's really likeable. Loveable???? To me???? I think maybe Yaz was right when she called him lover boy. I know that sounds silly.*
>
> *But how will I know if this is really love? Real. True. Love?*

Melody looked up and stared at wrinkled brown corduroy. Her eyes moved upward until she met her father's face. She noticed his eyes had that sparkly look he got when he was excited about something archeological. But his mouth was frowning.

"Why didn't you answer my texts? I didn't know where you were."

Melody squinted up at him and snapped her notebook shut.

"Okay, so how was your day, Mouse?"

"Fuck, Dad. Rodent?"

"Sorry, Melody. Watch your language."

"Watch yours."

Her father sat down in an adjacent chair and stared out at the sea of gray roofs and the golden dome in the distance. His hands gripped the sides of the chair. He turned toward her, his voice strained. "Reset? Let's have dinner and talk about our days." His head tilted hopefully, but Melody caught the slump in his shoulders.

Defeat. Why are we always fighting? When will he really get me? "Fine."

Her father smiled, relieved. "That's my girl." He stood up and extended his hand to pull her out of the chair.

Melody stood up by herself. *So not his girl. Who wears corduroy anyway? In this heat. It's so…medieval. And that vest. Thank god I won't meet anyone I know.*

Chapter Twelve

COUSINS

MELODY STEPPED OUT OF THE AIR-CONDITIONED TAXI, wilted slightly from the rush of hot air. She stared up at the old Ottoman era Clock Tower and the three palm trees standing stately at the end of the narrow plaza, then stretched her back and cracked her neck. *Too. Much. Sitting. And staring out the window. Clock's pretty cool. This country's like a fucking museum. In a barbeque.* She took a swig of water and popped the bottle into her backpack.

Melody cupped her hand over her eyes and scanned the crowd, looking for her cousin, Malkah. *What's she like? Will I hate her? Will she like me?* They had already exchanged photos; she knew Malkah would be wearing a floppy pink sunhat. *Pink? Really?* Just as she sat down on the stairs at the base of the tower, she saw a droopy hat with a bright purple flower waving and weaving through the crowds toward her.

"Melody?" pink hat yelled across the street. "Oh super, thought it was you." Pink hat waved excitedly.

Purple flower? That's so stupid. Here goes. Melody stood up, hesitated, then dashed between the oncoming motorbikes and cars; daredevil Hyundais and Toyotas vied for the narrow lanes. One driver stuck out her middle finger and another let loose with a string of angry Hebrew invective. *People here. Maniacs.* "Hi." Melody waved. "Malkah?"

Melody stopped as she reached the curb. A surge of anxiety nearly toppled her over. She looked at Malkah's pink nails and perfectly shaped, arched eyebrows. A large sparkling ring encircled her first finger. *Hollywood meets Valley Girl. Not. My. Style.*

Malkah also paused, looked her up and down, grinned, and gave her a hug. "Glad we found each other."

"Yeah," Melody said, shifting from one foot to the other. Uneasy.

"I can't believe your dad just lets you travel alone."

"Yeah. He doesn't care." She shrugged.

"How was the train ride?"

"Good. The high-speed train from Jerusalem was superfast."

"Too bad it only goes to the airport. You got the connecting train okay?"

Melody nodded. The conversation dwindled. *Awkward, awkward. It's hard to talk about the weather when it is just too hot all the time.*

"Well, let's get going. The beach is only a ten-minute walk. We'll just head toward that rotary thing," Malkah pointed, "and then it's a few blocks to the promenade and the water."

Melody nodded, relieved. *Something. To. Do.*

"I can't wait to show you the beach. It's really gorgeous. I can't believe it. You're here. In the flesh! Trust me. Summer has been so boring."

Melody smiled. Her father's voice echoed in her brain. "Be appropriate, she's family. She wants to meet you." *Just breathe. How painful could this be? It's a day at the beach. Just be friendly. I am friendly. Maybe a little less cursing. Okay, be civilized.*

"You thirsty?"

Melody shook her head no.

The cousins started walking, weaving between tourists and locals chattering in Hebrew and a smattering of Arabic. They passed a clutch of dogs encircling a dog walker, tails wagging like a row of metronomes. *We could talk dogs. That's a good topic.* Melody took out her phone and flipped through photos of Cheddar, holding them up for Malkah who stared through her wraparound sunglasses. Cheddar fetching a half-dead soccer ball. Cheddar, ears flopping wildly. Cheddar rolling on his back. Cheddar asleep on her bed.

Malkah giggled. "Super cool. I love dogs, but our apartment is too small, I mean for a big dog like that. Plus my mom hates them. Especially the barking."

Melody tried to nod sympathetically. "There's a cute little poodle." She pointed. When she spotted the turquoise water and flat sandy beach, her mouth gaped open. "Fuck me! Pretty spectacular. A-ma-zing."

Malkah laughed nervously, grabbed Melody's hand, and dragged her down the promenade toward the sand, heat emanating from the pavement. Melody inhaled the salty smell of the ocean. "This is gorgeous." She whirled around in the hot sun, holding on to her baseball cap. "I could definitely get used to this."

"How about here?" Malkah unrolled her beach towel and plopped down, patting the warm sand next to her.

Melody stood for a moment, taking in the gentle flat waves rolling in with a soothing rhythm, the gray high rises and Tel Aviv skyline to the north, and the ancient Clock Tower and old city of Jaffa tumbling down to the water to the south.

"Watch out." Malkah yelled as a Frisbee sailed by and Melody ducked. She waved at a very bronzed, muscular guy jogging toward her.

"Quite a hulk." A lively Labrador trotted after him. The girls wriggled out of their clothes and stretched out on their towels, slathering themselves with sunblock.

"I'll do your back," Malkah offered. Melody nodded, not sure how comfortable she felt with her cousin's hand circling over her shoulder blades. "Wow, you got a ton of freckles."

"Yup." Melody sighed. Her back stiffened. Freckles weren't her strong point. She looked at Malkah's smooth, browned skin. *The. Perfect. Tan.* "Shall I do yours?" Malkah pulled down her bikini straps.

As Melody rubbed her cousin's back, she felt her guard shifting, her tension sinking into the hot sand. She was churning with questions. *Could I really ask her? What could she tell me?* "It's cool to meet you. You were always my mysterious Israeli cousin, but you seem, like so American. Can I ask you something?"

"Sure."

"Okay, here goes." Melody took a deep breath. "I know our moms had some big fight when your mom decided to live here forever."

Malkah nodded.

"But, did she ever talk about my mom? What did your mom say about her? What was my mom like as a kid, her younger sister? Does she remember my mom meeting my dad? What did she look like? When…"

"You got some list! Are you looking for family secrets?" Malkah laughed.

"No, just general detective work." *Maybe a little less diarrhea of the mouth? Too pushy.* "She died before I could really get to know her. I mean, more than like a kid knows their mom. And the last few years were all chemo and radiation and that kind of crap."

"Yeah, my mom talks about her sister, your mom, a lot," Malkah said, suddenly serious. "I think your mom was five years younger than my mom, but when they were older, people thought they were twins."

Melody nodded. "Sounds right."

"They were really close when they were little, your mom called my mom, 'the boss.' My mom was like a little mother and your mom idolized her, until she decided to leave for Israel. That kinda changed everything. You know, different life choices. But lucky for me, 'cause I got born here." Malkah grinned and gave a thumbs up.

"Right. Lucky you." *Lucky you have a mom.* Melody listened carefully. She was hungry for details. *Dad is so frustrating, like a sphinx. Silent. At least Malkah's a talker.*

Sunbathers sprawled around them, some under white umbrellas, some baking in the sun. Little kids giggled and dug sandcastles, lapped by the waves. A woman in a hijab and loose white dress played in the water with her daughter beside women in skimpy bathing suits and tangled wet hair. Rock music throbbed from a nearby restaurant.

"Did you know your mom never learned to swim?" Malkah asked.

Melody nodded. "She used to tell me the story about how she almost drowned in a pool as a kid. All choking and barfing up water. She never put her foot in a body of water bigger than a bathtub, ever again. A really stubborn kid."

"And my mom tried to teach her, once she dragged her into a lake."

"Was that the time my mom bit your mom? I guess that was the end of swimming lessons."

"That's the family story," Melody agreed.

"But she wanted you to learn, right?'

"She always said I could do better than her," Melody smiled, "because I had a better mother."

"That's cute. I heard Grandma was a pretty crazy lady. Really nervous about everything. My mom says she yelled a lot too. Didn't approve of your dad, at all. You know, 'cause he wasn't Jewish."

"Right."

"Grandma forbid them from seeing each other, but your mom would sneak out if he was visiting when she was at home, or lie, say she was out with her girlfriends. Of course it was easier when they were at grad school on their own. At the same university."

"She was stubborn."

Malkah nodded toward the water. "It's hot. Wanna swim?"

"Sure. I did actually learn."

After a dip in the waves, the girls returned to their towels. "I can't wait for you to meet my big brother. You're gonna like him." Malkah made circles with her toe in the sand. "Hand me the sunblock again, will you?"

"So, what's he like?" Melody squirted some in her hand and tossed the bottle to her cousin. *This seemed like a safe topic.*

"Well, he's twenty and he's in the army. I'm sooo proud of him. Like he's in some intelligence unit or something. He can't tell me. It must be important secret stuff. But you'll see. He's really brave and really sweet."

"Brave and sweet? Not sure he's my type," joked Melody. She threw some sand at Malkah's feet.

"Oh, not in that way, he's your cousin for God's sake. But he has cute friends."

"So where is he now?"

"I bet he's at his apartment. He shares it with a bunch of guys in his unit."

"He doesn't live on a base?"

"Sunday morning he goes to the base and he comes back Thursday evening. They do army service like that for three years."

"Why's he in the army?" Melody adjusted her visor and looked closely at Malkah. "Doesn't he want to go to college or something?"

"In Israel, everyone serves in the army."

"Everyone?"

"Well, most kids, when we finish high school. It's just what we do, it's a law. And *then* we go to college. Or not," Malkah smiled. "I mean lots of my teachers are in the army and we go to summer programs on military bases. And our dads are in the reserves, they do military service every year, like for a month. It's just part of being…Israeli."

"Oh." Melody went silent and stared out at the Mediterranean Sea, a deep purple blue at the horizon, her eyes followed the crests of waves as they rippled across the expansive beach. *In general, not exactly a fan of the military. Keep that one private.*

"I got an idea. We're getting totally roasted out here." Malkah sounded excited. "Let me text him and see if we can drop by."

"You sure?"

"I'm sure. I think he would love to meet you, and I know he is off-duty today."

"I guess, since he's my cousin, I *should* meet him." Melody watched Malkah's thumbs fly, a scramble of Hebrew letters marched across the face of her phone. Minutes later she heard a familiar ping.

"He says, come over," announced Malkah.

"You sure?"

"Yes, let's do it."

The girls shook the sand off their feet and slipped into sandals. Melody held Malkah's towel loosely around her body as she pulled off her bathing suit bottoms. She wriggled into her short, cut-off jeans and wrangled her tank top over her head. "You got this down."

Malkah laughed, "I live on the beach. Now your turn." Melody wrapped her towel as Malkah grabbed it. As she pulled down her bottoms, she could feel the hot burning edges of her tan. Freckles blossomed across her face. If only I wasn't such a red head. *Thanks Dad,* she thought as she poked her head into the arm hole of her tee shirt. "Oops. Not as cool as you." She laughed as her elbows flailed under the towel. "Okay. Done."

Melody grabbed her baseball hat, stopped, and looked closely at Malkah's face, the familiar coffee-colored eyes, curly brown hair. Or was it something about her nose. "Shit. You know, I can really see my mom in your face," she said softly. Her tears simmered and she rubbed her eyes. *I am not gonna cry.* "It's just a little bit creepy." She grabbed a tissue from her backpack and blew her nose loudly. "I look so much like my dad. The hair and all."

"That's what happens when you marry a Sullivan," smirked Malkah.

"Gimme a break." Melody gave Malkah a friendly shove. "I got half my DNA from my mom. My dad likes to say her chromosomes just got overwhelmed by all those little Irish sperm. The fightin' Irish."

"That's gross." Malkah made a face and wrinkled her nose. "I never want to think about my parents, you know, doing it."

"Oh come on, how do you think we got here?"

Malkah moved her face close to Melody's. "Having in-ter-course." She spit out each syllable. "That's how."

"Oh, very good. How very mature you've become and such excellent language skills."

"Thanks, cuz." Malkah snatched Melody's hand and tugged. "Come on. We gotta walk back to the Clock Tower to get the bus."

Next adventure. Here goes. Melody shoved her hat over her sandy curls.

The girls grabbed their bags and started up the promenade. Soon they were stepping into a lumbering white bus with large windows and heading south, past upscale restaurants, funky artist studios, and gentrified apartments. When the neighborhood got distinctly less upscale, Malkah said, "Here's our stop."

They headed down a narrow, winding street, trash tumbling along the walls, cars parked half-way up the sidewalk, and stopped at a gray-blue door. Malkah rang the bell. Moments later, a tall young man with coffee-colored eyes and curly brown hair appeared at the door and motioned them to come upstairs to the apartment. Melody felt a little itchy from the salt and the sand. She smiled hesitantly, suddenly uncomfortable. She rubbed her nose ring and waited.

"Come in, come in," Daniel said. "You are the infamous little cousin from America. Come, meet the guys."

They walked up the uneven stairs and into a small living room, old couches covered with Indian bedspreads and a battered coffee table in the center, cluttered with beer bottles and a swirly blue glass pipe, ashes scattered. Melody noticed a faded Beatles poster tacked to the wall next to some Israeli band she did not recognize and inhaled the pungent smell of weed. Two guys in jeans and tee shirts sprawled across the couches, their assault rifles leaning up against the wall nearby.

"This is my cousin Melody, from the States," said Daniel to his buddies. "Meet Shlomo and Dov, guys in my unit. Melody is staying in Jerusalem while her dad does some kind of conference."

"Archeology," Melody added, holding on to her towel.

"We're all having dinner tonight at my parents' place. Come sit," Daniel gestured toward the couch. "There's plenty of room. How 'bout you put your butt down between Shlomo and Dov."

Shlomo sat up and smoothed the bedspread. "Would you like a toke?" He reached for a cigarette lighter and clicked. The flame flickered as he put the pipe to his lips.

Melody looked at Malkah. Malkah laughed. "He's my brother's friend. It's okay." She reached out for the pipe, inhaled deeply and handed it to Melody. A whisp of smoke drifted from the bowl.

"I'm really not sure," Melody said. *I am so out of my league.*

"Oh go ahead. You're in Israel. It's a fun place. Beautiful beaches, beautiful girls, excellent weed," said Dov winking. He wrapped his arm over her shoulder. Melody stiffened. *Just get over yourself. Just get along. He's Daniel's friend.*

Melody smiled an anxious, goofy grin and wrinkled her nose. "Okay." Her voice sounded higher and tighter than she expected. She leaned forward away from Dov, took the pipe and inhaled deeply, but started coughing immediately. Malkah handed her a half-full bottle of beer. "Drink, it'll help. Don't do this much? Huh?"

Melody laughed, gave her a wide-eyed nod, and sank into the couch, feeling a buzz and pleasantly high. She gulped the beer. The cool liquid felt good on her throat.

"So, where are you from?" asked Shlomo.

Melody heard his question and struggled to focus. "Vermont, I'm from Vermont. My dad teaches at a college there, ancient archeology of the Middle East." Suddenly that seemed very funny, and she started to giggle.

"Good stuff, huh. Have another puff, melodious Melody," said Dov.

"Oh-My-God. I can't tell you how many kids have called me melodious, so just don't." Dov put his hands together and bowed slightly. Melody tipped her head, smiled, took the pipe and drew in another breath, holding it longer this time, until she started hacking again.

"Be careful, Melody. This stuff is crazy potent." Malkah wiggled in and sat down next to her and touched her knee.

Daniel stood up and ambled down a long corridor to the kitchen. He came back with a large bag of chips and a tub of hummus. "So how do you find Jerusalem?"

Melody felt herself floating and stared intently at the Beatles poster, "Sgt. Pepper's Lonely Hearts Club Band." She felt the lonely hearts part spoke to her in some special way. She fixated on John's yellow jacket and the way his hand gripped the French horn. "Jerusalem? It's very…" Her mind went blank. "Old."

Malkah gave her a quizzical look. "Girl, you are very stoned. No more for you." Melody started laughing again. She felt so light. The patterns in the covers on the couch seemed vivid and distracting. She struggled to focus on the conversation, a blur of English and Hebrew, something about the beach and a possible hike and a good burger joint in Tel Aviv.

Melody reached for the chips and crunched a handful in her mouth. "Do they have cheeseburgers here?" Suddenly she needed to pee. Urgently. She whispered to Malkah. "Where's the bathroom?"

Malkah pointed toward the hall. "All the way down at the end. You okay?"

"Yeah, okay." Melody extracted herself from the couch and got up, feeling a bit wobbly. She peered down a long, dimly lit narrow hall. As she walked slowly, her hand gliding along the wall, she noticed a row of film posters, Gal Gadot, her Wonder Woman hair flying, breasts full and shining in golden armor. The actress stood fiercely, legs spread, wielding a sword and shield, and stared seductively at Melody. Suddenly, she felt the heat of Dov beside her.

"Pretty sexy lady. You know, she was a combat instructor in the army."

Melody turned to face him. "Really?" She stared at a pimple erupting on his chin. He was that close.

"Really. My kinda woman. Hey, you want to party?"

"What?"

He pressed her against the wall and reached under her shirt, grabbing her breast.

"Hey. What the fuck. Get off me." Melody's heart thumped hard in her chest. Her brain exploded.

"I know you'll like this." He pressed his face against hers and shoved his tongue into her mouth, his free hand wrapped around her neck.

Melody smelled his smoky, hummus breath and pushed him with everything she had. A muffled shriek came out of her mouth.

Dov slapped his hand over her mouth. "Man, don't ruin it. Don't you find soldiers…sexy?" He shoved his hand under her blouse, pressed against her other breast and leaned into her. She could feel his erection bulging, his pelvis rocking against her, her buttocks rhythmically smacking the wall.

"Oh baby…"

Melody squirmed against his muscled grip and fiercely kicked his shin.

Daniel suddenly appeared. "Hey man, get off her. She's a kid."

Dov moved away, caught his breath. "Shit." He glared at her. "Shit."

Daniel looked at Melody as she backed down the hall, shaking. Vomit rose in her mouth, converging with the sour taste of Dov's tongue.

"You okay?"

"Fucking no." She squinted her eyes at him and glared. "Your so-called friends really suck. Suck big time. Where's that bathroom?"

Daniel pointed to the end of the hall. "Sorry about that. He's pretty stoned."

"That's not an excuse. Fuck you." Melody hurried down the hall and locked herself in the tiny bathroom. Her exploding bladder released as she sat on the toilet, face cupped in her hands, and cried. "What is wrong with these people?" She took a deep breath and rocked back and forth. A sob escaped from somewhere deep inside her. "Mom, Mom, Mom, what should I do?" Tears flooded her eyes and she wrapped her arms around her shoulders, hugging herself, feeling a stab of loneliness and fear. A drop of snot dripped off her nose ring. She unrolled some toilet paper and blew her nose hard.

She leaned back against the toilet, shaking, and took a slow deep breath. *I have to get out of here.* Began singing "Sgt. Pepper's Lonely Hearts Club Band" in a low, hoarse whisper of a voice. She just wanted to crawl inside the song and let the evening go.

"I need a shower. Oh God, what a bastard." She heard a knock on the door, it was Malkah.

"Hey, Melody, you okay in there?"

Reluctantly she stood up, pulled up her jeans, wiped her nose again with the back of her hand, and unlocked the door. Her left nipple throbbed painfully.

"No. Get me out of here."

Malkah gasped. "Oh God. Did he?"

Melody glared.

Malkah grabbed her hand. "Let's go."

Chapter Thirteen

TOTALLY FUCKED

MELODY CLICKED THE LOCK ON THE BATHROOM door at Malkah's apartment and leaned against the gray tiled wall, sinking against a row of green towels. During the bus ride with Malkah, she had sat in total silence. A mix of anger and hurt. Malkah thankfully silent.

She took out her phone and texted Yasmina. *Yaz, I need to talk to you. NOW.*

She turned to the sink and stared at her face, pink cheeks, freckles, smudged mascara. "God, I look like shit. Why me?"

She could hear her aunt chattering in Hebrew, the clink of glasses and plates on a table. Malkah's laughter. An Israeli band in the background. She splashed water on her face, rubbed her skin vigorously with soap, and opened the medicine cabinet, searching for mouthwash.

Dental floss? No. Paracetamol? No. Ah, toothpaste. Yes.

Melody looked at her phone. No response. She pressed some toothpaste on her finger, scrubbed her teeth and gargled, but the sour, smoky taste lingered in her throat. She texted again.

Yasmina, answer me!!!! ☺, 🦋

She heard the doorbell ring. Her father's deep voice, the sounds of welcome. Hugs. A chair scraping on the floor. The phone pinged and Melody jumped. It was Aaron.

Hi. How ya doin?

"Shit." Melody dried her face and took a deep breath.

Can't talk now. She pushed send. Then her thumbs tapped. *Thanks for asking.* She searched for an emoji. 🏝, 📳

Her phone pinged again. *U OK?* 📳, 🤍

She searched for a smiley face.

Melody propped her butt against the sink and tried to steady herself. *I so don't want to be here.* Hiding in the bathroom, she heard the front door open again. Daniel's voice.

"So nice to meet you, you're Melody's father? Hi, Mom. I can smell the kebabs. Excellent choice." Back slapping, kissing. "Give our visitors a taste of your great Israeli cooking. And here's my father, having a smoke, as usual. Dad, you know that will kill you." Loud chuckle. More back slapping. "How ya doin'?"

The phone pinged. Melody stared at the screen. Yasmina.

Not now. Maybe later. Sorry.

I need to talk now. Why why why????

Trouble here. Worse than expected. Really bad.

What?

My uncle.

What happened?

Tear gassed.

Is he okay?

In the hospital. Long story.

Melody stared at her phone. She tried to wrap her mind around the word tear gas, which floated into tears, teary, tearful. She grabbed a tissue and blew her nose. In the hospital?

Are you okay Yaz? Is he okay? She bit her lip.

Don't worry about us. Love you.

"This sucks," Melody muttered. She nibbled on her fingernail. "A lonely and dangerous world, kiddo." She leaned forward and kissed her silver bracelet, the string of emeralds, smooth on her lips. Soothing. She thought about all the times her mother called her kiddo. *I'm your kiddo, Mom. I'm your totally fucked kiddo.*

Melody took a deep breath, ran her fingers through her hair, and squashed her baseball cap over the curls. She could smell the odor of Dov and weed on her clothes. "Shit." She unclicked the lock and turned the doorknob. "Hi Dad," she said flatly.

Her dad smiled. "How was your day at the beach? Isn't Malkah a sweetie?"

As Malkah and her mother laid out platters of olives, chopped tomatoes, baba ganoush, and tabbouleh, Melody felt herself floating into the room, almost as if she were on the wrong end of a telescope and everyone was getting smaller and smaller.

Malkah walked up to her and whispered. "Hey. My father would kill me if he knew I was at my brother's house. I'm not supposed to go over there. He doesn't want me smoking."

Melody stared at the smiling faces, the generous dinner, the cactus potted in the corner, the shelves of books and DVDs, the photo of the family smiling on a Tel Aviv beach. She turned to her cousin and nodded. "Sure." She felt numb, like someone had shoved a blow dryer into her mouth, like she was turning to stone. *Didn't someone turn to stone in the Bible? Or was that a horror movie?* She spotted a tiny ceramic bowl filled with salt. *Oh yeah, maybe it was salt, some lady turned to salt.*

She stared at Daniel. His voice seemed far away. Malkah laughed loudly and shoved her brother as their conversation lapsed into Hebrew. Melody felt like she was hovering over the dinner table, there, but not really there. She heard her father ask Daniel, something about his life as a soldier. She heard him respond, something about the camaraderie on his base, the importance of the work, the dangers of patrolling Arab cities, especially Hebron, especially now. So many Jewish settlers to protect. Religious sites. So many angry, out-of-control Arabs. She felt suddenly alert. *Hebron? Where Yasmina and her family live? Dangers? He and his buddies…the Israeli soldiers in Hebron.* Her jaw clenched. *Did they tear gas Yaz's uncle???*

She sat down at the dinner table, feeling stunned and confused, bewildered by this new piece of the family puzzle. She asked herself, *Whose side are you on? Do I have to take sides?* Then the memories of the day jittered into her head like a song on rewind. The glorious beach, the sun, the weed, the hand crushing her breast, the terror. *Was it what I was wearing?* She stared down at her loose tee shirt, her nipples easily visible. *The tee shirt? Oh I should never have gotten stoned. Did he think I was asking for it? Stationed in Hebron? Really?*

Chapter Fourteen

PANIC

MELODY'S MOUTH FELT CARDBOARD DRY AS SHE suddenly opened her eyes and let out a desperate scream. "No!" She sat up abruptly and looked around. Her dream wafted into her consciousness like a cloud of drifting smoke. She was floating on a calm Mediterranean ocean, swayed by the waves. Friendly dolphins cavorted nearby, sea gulls swooped and squawked, when suddenly a toothy shark with a man's face grabbed her leg and pulled her under. "I can't breathe, Mama, Mama," she gasped. She took a deep breath and sat up. "Okay, I can breathe." She touched her bracelet. "It's morning. Hi, Mom." *Jerusalem. No sharks. Inhale.*

She looked around the room, trying to calm herself. The pale, flowery wallpaper, high arches, darkly stained headboard and closet doors felt ancient and strangely comforting. Floor to ceiling mustard-colored curtains pooled on the marble floor blocking the light. A faded picture of the Al Aqsa Mosque and Dome of the Rock stared down at her father's rumpled, unmade sheets on an adjacent bed. She spotted a note propped up on his oversized white pillow, leaned over, and grabbed it.

> Morning, Mouse. Hope you got a good sleep. You look so peaceful lying in that bed. Reminded me of old times. You seemed so quiet last night. You didn't eat much. Still jet lagged? Stomach upset? Hope you feel better. See you tonight for dinner. I've got a really authentic old Jerusalem restaurant in mind. Enjoy your big explore today. xoxoxo

Melody stretched and then swung her feet onto the cool floor. "Mouse? Really, Dad." Another day. Abandoned. She yawned. *I can't stand to be alone and I can't trust anyone. Anyone here. Who am I ever gonna hang with?* She spotted the hotel brochure lying on the night table.

> The HaShimi Guesthouse: in the heart of the Old
> City of Jerusalem…beautiful roof top terrace with
> magnificent views of the city… The building is over 500 years
> old… a perfect place to relax after a long day sightseeing.…

A perfect place to hide from sharks, she thought as she headed for the shower. "What's with the water pressure around here? Original Biblical plumbing? Did they even have plumbing?" She grabbed the Dead Sea Mineral soap and scrubbed her body vigorously under the slow trickle of not-quite-hot-enough water. "Oh, I just feel so…I don't know, dirty. What a disgusting feeling." She grabbed a washcloth and rubbed frantically until her skin hurt. She just wanted to scour off the memory of Dov's hard penis. Pressing into her. Water dripped from the Star of David around her neck and trickled toward her tanned, freckled belly.

She slipped on a black tee shirt and jeans as her empty stomach growled for attention. "I wish I had my see-no-evil sports bra. Well, I don't. God, my nipples are still sore." She toweled her rambunctious hair and tossed her head back and forth. "Okay. Let's see if I cope with today. Maybe I should eat something first." She and her therapist had talked endlessly about "coping strategies." None of them felt like good enough for today.

Her toe hit a folded note lying on the floor near the closet. She bent down, picked it up, and walked over to the bed, her heart suddenly thudding. A premonition. Something her oh so scatter-brained father misplaced? Dropped as he tiptoed out of the room before she woke up? She scanned the Hebrew writing across the top, probably some hotel address, maybe something from his meetings. She grasped the note firmly as she read, the left-handed script slanting dramatically backwards.

Dear Philly,

So great to see you after all these years, can't believe we ended up at the same conference, small world if I must say. I just loved chatting with you after that last sleep-inducing lecture, *the best Mojitos I've had in a long time* - really brought back the old days. Remember that bar with the great blues band!!! Gotta admit, you are still charming *as in you still make my heart throb* ☺

Hope we can see more of each other.

xoxo
Lydia
212-547-3232

"Philly?" Melody collapsed onto the bed. "Lydia? Who the fuck is that?" Melody reread the note, her eyes stopping at "heart throb." "Some old girlfriend from the dark ages? I can't believe my father." Melody closed her eyes, rocked back and forth. *Oh Mom. How could he do this to you?*

Her phone pinged, and she saw a text from Malkah. She exhaled loudly. *My life is a shit show. I'm definitely looooosing it.*

Talk?

Melody did not respond. Her head suddenly throbbed. *She may be the last person in the world I ever want to see.*

Please, I'm sorry.

Melody stopped and debated for a moment. *I don't have to talk to her. But she is my cousin. But it was her creepy brother's best friend.* As her thoughts turned to Daniel's apartment, her stomach turned and she felt a surge of nausea. *No. No. No.*

Please????

She stared at the note from Lydia, crumpled it in her fist, and heaved it across the room. It hit the wall with a boink and rolled into a corner. She let out one growling scream, "Enough!" and flopped straight out on the bed, staring at the ceiling.

"I've got to see Yaz." She cupped her phone and texted Yasmina.

Come to Jerusalem. I really need you!!!!

Melody grabbed a pillow and hugged it tightly. She waited, concentrating on slow breathing. The air felt thick. She squeezed her eyes closed and placed one hand on her belly, rising and falling. Her breath slowly in and out. She felt her panic gripping her.

Can't.

WHY WHY WHY???

She stared at her phone, waiting anxiously. Her hand shook.

The soldiers are crazy here.

So????

Another pause.

Mel, I gotta stay with my family.

Melody sat up. *I thought I was your family too!!!!*

Can't leave. No permit.

Soul sister????

There's too much trouble here. Plus I CAN'T. Get it?

Well, I have trouble too!!!!

"God damn it," she muttered. She threw her phone into her lap, tears rising like an unwelcomed explosion. Yasmina's absence felt like a huge void, like Melody was sinking into a weird abyss. Her heart lurched, and a bead of sweat broke out on her forehead. *Oh god, I'm falling. I've got to…Get Outside. Walk. Breathe.*

Her dad's words suddenly pierced her thoughts. "You're old enough to be more independent than you think."

"Oh right," Melody snorted. She felt hurt and needy and little. A wave of defiance and rage swept her body.

"Well, if she can't come to me…then I'll just… go to her," she said out loud, stopping to feel the weight of her thoughts. *Why should I even tell Dad? He could care less. He's got a heart throb for Christ sake.*

She stood up and buckled her belt. *This is a really bad idea. Tear gas? Soldiers? Daniel and his buddies? With their guns? Don't. Be. Stupid.*

"Why the fuck not?" She took a very deep breath and exhaled, like she was blowing dragon fire. *If Yaz can be there, then why can't I be there?*

Melody grabbed her key, slammed the door, and headed down the steep hotel stairs onto the narrow stone cobbled street. A faint mustiness filled her nostrils. Old and damp. Nobody even glanced her way. *I am utterly, totally alone.*

She bolted into the crowds, her heart pounding, and found herself in a dim covered walkway crowded with shoppers that opened onto Damascus Gate. She shielded her eyes as she came through the massive doorway into the light and the big open plaza. She felt clobbered by her rushing pulse and a wave of trembling when she spotted a cluster of Israeli soldiers loitering on the stairs, casually holding assault rifles, chatting, smiling. *Guns? Everywhere?* Women in loose hijabs and abayas sat on the walkway hawking piles of fresh thyme and basil. *Everybody looks like they think this is normal. How could this be normal? Am I crazy?*

Melody lowered herself onto the wide plaza steps, leaning against a stone wall. *Inhale. Exhale. Just like the shrink said.* She grabbed her hands and pressed them against her chest, trying to stop the shaking. She tried singing "Sgt. Pepper," but no sound came out, the words just rattled in her brain.

Melody leaned back and stared at the hustle in front of her. She felt her pulse gradually slowing in the warmth of the sun. *Here come the freckles.* She sighed deeply and opened her pack, retrieved her guidebook, and thumbed through Jerusalem bus service, stared at a map of Hebron. *I just don't get it. Arab bus station???*

> Passengers take **bus** to Bethlehem from the **Arab bus** station in Damascus Gate in **Jerusalem**. These buses depart frequently, and the trip from Jerusalem to Bethlehem should take about 45 minutes and cost about seven shekels. This **bus** goes to **Bethlehem** 300 Checkpoint as the last station.
>
> In Bethlehem, internationals will likely be greeted by numerous taxi drivers. You may take a private taxi for about $25 (not more than 100 NIS) the rest of the way to Hebron.
>
> The checkpoint is usually filled with many yellow service minivans. Ask for the service to Hebron. The service to Hebron generally costs nine shekels (9 NIS).

Melody reached into her pack, took out a small leather pouch, and pulled out a fold of shekels. She searched the bottom of her bag for loose change, and started counting. *Okay, so I have 72 shekels, I could do this.* She sat for a while staring at the massive stone gate, determination swelling inside of her, then stood up impulsively. "Excuse me, do you speak English?"

An older woman stopped.

"Where is the Arab bus station?" She pointed to the left, where Melody saw a cluster of buses and people. "Thank you. I mean, toda." Melody reached for her Star of David and stuffed the necklace under her shirt. She squirmed as the necklace wiggled between her breasts. Then she turned to the left and walked directly toward the buses.

Chapter Fifteen

FEAR AND DEFIANCE

MELODY SHOOK HER HEAD AT A TAXI DRIVER accosting her in a hopeful clamor for business as she dodged between the cars. *Lunatics.* She stopped on the other side of the street and spotted two neatly bearded Israeli soldiers who strode right in front of her; she could almost touch their assault rifles. *They look like college kids back home. Armed.* As that thought percolated in her brain, she noticed a young man in tight jeans, wearing a keffiyeh around his neck, spread-eagled against a building. He was being frisked by two thirty-something border police in body armor and helmets, their batons menacing in their backpacks. *Yasmina said there was too much trouble in Hebron. What the hell is going on right here? In Israel? In Jerusalem?*

Melody bit her lip anxiously as she approached the bus station, rows of white busses parked in front of covered roofs; lines of people stood between metal fences leading to each bus. She noticed bored drivers leaning against open doors, smoking cigarettes, chatting in Arabic on cellphones. She spotted the yellow metal sign to Bethlehem, checkpoint 300, and got in line.

Melody's defiance faded as she reached the driver and handed him her shekels. She moved slowly down the aisle and deliberately scooted across two seats to the window. Holding her backpack on her lap, the FIGHT POVERTY NOT WAR sticker had partially torn off, leaving a ragged NOT WAR.

Melody reached into her backpack, pulled out her notebook and pen, and leaned it on the pack. *I can do this.* She stared at the old sticker, flipped through the pages of her writing until she reached a fresh sheet of paper. Melody gazed at the blankness of the page and drew a stick-figure wonder woman gripping a sword.

Page seven

Flying like a bird
Going where I need to go
A fish moving upstream
Against the wild river flow.

Feeling wonder woman strong
In the crazy after glow
Of Aaron's sweetest messages,

She looked out the window, playing with a rhyme for "glow," when a middle-aged woman slid next to her. Melody turned and spotted a gold cross draped around her neck, peeking through the fold of her loose gray blouse. *Another believer?* The woman smiled, and Melody smiled weakly back. She tapped her thumb and first finger on the page.

Her pulse quickened, and she tried a few deep inhales as she watched the passengers climbing on board, young women in hijabs and loose coats, others in more Western dress, older men in suits, mothers holding squirming children, a priest with wire-rimmed glasses. *Exhale, slowly.* She listened to the quiet chatter in Arabic, wishing she had a clue to the conversations. She reread her poem. *Gotta find that last line. Low? Foe? Grow? Know?*

The engine started up, and the bus lumbered out of the station. Melody stared at the cream-colored stone buildings slipping by as they approached the highway, her face reflected in the glass. She caught sight of apartment buildings, hotels, patches of green shrubs, a huge mall, the bustle of people and cars. Her fingers started tapping again, a rhythmic, anxious beat. The bus sped in and out of tunnels, the light and dark flickering on her poem.

Melody was jolted out of her quiet turmoil when the lady next to her offered her a piece of sesame candy. "Thanks." She unwrapped the candy. "Do you speak English?" She looked at her expectantly.

"My dear, I do." The woman nodded. "Where are you from?"

A real person I can talk to. Who calls me "dear". Thank god. "I'm from the US. Do you know Vermont?"

The woman smiled. "I have cousins in Vermont."

"Really? You do?" Melody's eyebrows shot up and then she relaxed into her seat, dropped her notebook into her backpack, and slid it between her knees, down to the floor. She felt a rush of excitement and relief. *This could be interesting.* "So you're from Israel?"

"No, no. East Jerusalem. Why are you here?"

"Oh." Melody felt bewildered. "My dad's at an archeology conference. He's a professor. So I'm just here with him. I guess he didn't know what else to do with me."

"And your mom?"

"She's dead." Melody bit her lip. The conversation paused and Melody felt a pang of regret. "I mean, she died when I was younger. Breast cancer."

"I'm so sorry."

"It's okay. I'm kind a used to it."

"That's a hard thing to get used to. I'm a nurse, I've seen a lot of death. It is never easy. I live in Jerusalem, the Arab side of Jerusalem, but I work in Bethlehem."

"Oh, so you take this bus a lot?"

"Five days a week, sometimes six."

Melody thought about this for a minute. "And you have an ID?"

"I have a Jerusalem ID, so I can travel back and forth."

Shit, I knew this would be complicated. "Can I see it?"

"My name is Khulood, by the way." She opened her purse and took out a plastic blue folder with the Israeli Coat of Arms embossed on the outer cover and the words TRAVEL DOCUMENT. "And I always travel with this, too." She handed Melody a document for The Hashemite Kingdom of Jordan, embossed with some kind of royal symbol and the word PASSPORT.

Melody smiled for the first time and laughed. "Well, I'm Melody, and this is as clear as mud."

"It is confusing. The blue one means I am a permanent resident of East Jerusalem, which is occupied by Israel, so I can come and go without a special permit. Many Palestinians also have a Jordanian passport, but we are not citizens of Jordan. More confusing, right? It's important for us to always carry our IDs. It's a long story."

"I'm sure it's very, very long." Melody sighed. She thought of Yasmina. "But, let's say you lived in Hebron. What then?"

"It gets complicated. Palestinians in Hebron have green ID cards, and they have to get a permit to cross into Jerusalem, which is almost impossible. Especially now with the street protests."

"Street protests?" Melody gulped. Her phone started pinging. "I'm sorry, I gotta check this."

She stared at her phone. Aaron.

How ya doing? Thinkin' of u. Cheddar's great. This a good time? Having fun?

Her thumbs flew across the screen. *I'm on a bus.*

Bus? Where to? Beach? Some place really old? Biblical? Masada? With Malkah? Tell me tell me.

Not exactly.

What does that mean?

Going someplace really old. Biblical.

U being cagey? Where?

To Bethlehem. Going to Hebron, see Yaz.

What? Are u nuts?

Maybe.

Does your father know???

Course not.

He'll be so mad.

So what. Don't care.

He's your father!!!! Those people are Arabs. THEY HATE JEWS.

Shut up.

No really, they kill Jews. Famous massacre!!!!

Please don't.

U don't get it. Arabs want to destroy Israel. Not safe there – on their side of the fence.

What about Yaz??? You like her.

Always exceptions. She's a good Arab. Maybe family okay. BUT U DON'T KNOW THEM!!!

Melody put the phone down and stared out the window. Ping, ping.

Mel, u paying attention? This is serious. Hear everything from my cousin. In the IDF. He knows. Lives in Kiryat Arba, right next to Hebron. Those Arabs are animals.

Melody sighed and glared at the phone.

Mel...Don't know what to say. Sooo freakin freaked!!!!

Aaron, chill. Nice nurse lady just gave me candy. NO ONE WANTS TO KILL ME. She searched for an emoji. ☺, 👍

Don't joke. Hebron. Really dangerous!!!!   , 😈

Melody felt exhausted. *We'll see. Don't worry about me. B fine.*

Melody, I care about u!!! Of course I worry.

Melody stared at the phone. Another ping.

💜

She shoved the phone into her backpack as Aaron kept texting. *He's really freaking. What have I gotten myself into? Street protests?* She bit her lip.

Khulood patted Melody's arm. "Is your friend upsetting you?"

Melody looked at Khulood, tears rimming her eyes. She felt little and scared and angry. She took out her phone and showed Khulood the texts.

"Look dear, your friend cares about you but he doesn't know any better. Do the people in this bus look like monsters?"

Melody shook her head. She took off her baseball cap, ran her fingers through her hair, and scratched her head, curls flopping everywhere, as she scanned the passengers.

"Right now I want you to text your friend in Hebron and tell her what you have done. It would be best for someone to meet you at the check-point. And when we get to the checkpoint, just follow me. It's usually easy to get in. The soldiers only make it difficult when we want to get out. You have your passport, right?"

Melody nodded. *Out would be good, out would be very, very good.*

"And let your father know where you are."

Melody took out her phone. Her thumbs started tapping.

Yaz, I'm coming now.

DON'T. NOT NOW!!!

Already on my way. Meet me in Bethlehem, Checkpoint 300.

Melody's hand shook. Dad, not meeting u for dinner. Will explain.

Chapter Sixteen

EVERYTHING SCARES ME

"KHULOOD, AARON CALLED IT A *fence*!" Melody stared at the huge wall of concrete as the bus turned into the checkpoint, her nose almost pressed against the window. She felt her pulse thumping in her head. *That wall looks like a fucking prison.* She looked around at the other passengers in the bus; no one seemed anxious or even surprised. *So this is normal?* Melody took out her phone and snapped pictures through the window. *Wait 'til Aaron sees this.*

She focused on a discordant blue and white sign: PEACE BE WITH YOU. *Peace? Really? Not exactly.*

Khulood grabbed her arm and pushed it down. "Don't do that dear, this is a military terminal. You don't want to annoy the Israeli soldiers."

"Oh, right, that was dumb." Melody stuck her phone into her pack and blushed. "What would they do…if they saw me?" She pulled her baseball cap down to cover her face a bit. *Should I be scared? Or am I just plain stupid?* She tugged on her cap.

"Ah, my dear. They might yell, delete your photos, confiscate your phone. They could arrest you, send you back to Jerusalem…depending on their mood."

"Their mood?" Her mind flashed forward: her father storming into some dismal basement prison cell to find her, handcuffed and hungry. She could see the headlines in the college newspaper back home: Sixteen-year-old Daughter of College Professor Arrested on Spy Charges in Israel. *That would get his attention.*

"Dear, Bethlehem is a walled city, under occupation. We live and breathe at the whim and will of the soldiers. They're mostly young boys and girls, not much older than you. But they have huge power over our lives. Every day can be a surprise." Khulood smiled. "But you're an American, you'll be okay."

Soldiers. Whim and will. Right. Melody felt a new bolt of anxiety. She grabbed her silver bracelet and pressed her fingers around it and stared at her wrist. *Stay away from the handcuffs, okay?*

"Come, let's go." Khulood snatched Melody's hand and motioned to her to leave the bus with the other passengers. They walked up a steep, concrete, covered passageway into the checkpoint, through a gate, and began threading into lines, guided by blue metal fencing.

Melody stared open-mouthed at the soldiers watching overhead, automatic rifles pointed down at the travelers below. She felt bewildered, but Khulood gestured for her to push through a six-foot high, narrow steel turnstile into another queue. The light on the turnstile turned red-green-red-green, closed-open-closed-open. Melody waited for the green and pushed. On her third attempt, she heard a welcome click and felt the smooth steel bar against her skin. A voice in Hebrew barked from a loudspeaker in a control room somewhere. Melody looked around, trying to figure out where the voice came from. *Who controlled the red-green?*

People were pressed against other travelers, all waiting. Her calves and lower back tightened up from the anxious standing still. The sweaty smell of day laborers mixed with the perfume of an elegant woman in a wide hat standing in an expanse of multicolored hijabs. Melody looked at the faces around her and felt a mix of tension and resignation. Unlit cigarettes hung from the lips of some of the men. A heavily armed soldier leaned up against a white wall, scanning the crowd, gripping his automatic weapon, deliberately chewing gum. Melody looked up and noticed cameras everywhere. *It is a fucking prison.*

Khulood leaned toward her and said in a low voice, "See those new gates, they're called smart gates and they read biometric IDs. You know, the ones with the computer chips in them."

"Like…for cats and dogs?" Melody asked, confused. "I mean except they're not like *under* the skin."

"Sort of, but these are ID cards for people, the data is in the plastic card. Getting through is quicker if you have one. Just put down your card and do your fingerprint. But there's no way to escape the ugliness. The soldiers can still slow everything down, turn anyone away."

"Whim?"

Khulood nodded. "And of course, track everyone's location."

"Big brother?"

"I saw one guy who had calluses on his finger and they wouldn't let him through cause the machine couldn't read his fingerprint…

but all his permits were in order. Maybe big brother with a bad temper." Khulood smiled. "It is so frustrating and such a waste of time. But no worry, dear, we'll get through. They only screen people going *into* Jerusalem." Khulood nodded and reached for Melody's hand.

As they waited in line for the turnstile, Melody stared at the people trying to get back into Jerusalem on the other side of the adjacent half wall. A long line facing her, men and women carrying bags, children, their faces quiet and grim. She heard soldiers yelling and loud voices on the speakers.

"Ledaber Anglit? Speak English?"

"Empty pockets."

Melody listened carefully.

"Lo, lo, you cannot take that."

She heard a loud clunk into a trash bin, a pleading voice. "But I bought that for my boyfriend."

From another line, "You like Israel?"

Brief silence, what was the girl saying?

"You like Arabs?"

A stuttered, "I, I...I like everyone."

"You Jewish?"

"Sort of, yah, Well, my mom..."

"Rabbi's name?"

"No rabbi."

"Big mistake. Put your hands out. Separate legs," the soldier commanded.

Melody cringed at the thought of a security guard sweeping her hands over the girl's body, touching her.

"Yallah! Go!"

Another voice, "Go back, go back."

"Please, I need to visit my grandmother, she's dying."

"No. Yalla. Go." The sound of a suitcase dragging on the ground.

"Take off your jacket. Lift up your shirt. Turn around. Slowly."

An alarm clanged. "Take your suitcase off the conveyor belt. Come with me."

"ID?"

"Where are you going? ID?"

A chorus of barking dogs. With guns. They act like everyone is out to kill them. But the people around me, they seem like…regular folks. Like Khulood. Unarmed. Trying to get to work or something.

A baby shrieked. A woman shushed and spoke softly in Arabic. Children whined.

Melody closed her eyes briefly, exhaled loudly, and walked through the turnstile. *I'm a kid. Guns scare me. People with guns scare me. Everything scares me.* She hung her backpack across one shoulder. *Just think wonder woman.*

Melody scanned the corridor for Khulood who was standing quietly nearby.

"Why are the people going into Jerusalem getting so much," Melody searched for the word, "attention." *Jeez, I'm getting that zombie feeling again. Creepy, floaty, numb. UGHH. Not a good time for that.*

Melody bit her lip and followed Khulood into more queues and through more narrow, six-foot high turnstiles until they emerged onto a walkway with a corrugated metal roof, the wall of the checkpoint on one side, a four foot high concrete wall with vertical bars on the other. Khulood turned to Melody. "You okay habibti?"

Melody took a deep breath. "Sorry. That's a pretty creepy, scary place. All the soldiers, yelling, people being turned away."

"Well, dear. Now you have a tiny taste of what we Palestinians deal with every day. And you are an American, a white American girl. No problem. Plus they're not going to bother you – you're leaving Israel."

Melody nodded.

"Dear, thousands of workers gather on the Bethlehem side at 3:00 every morning to get through this checkpoint to their jobs in Israel. They often wait for hours."

"Hours?"

She shook her head. "Can you imagine? The daily humiliation? These men need to work to support their families. Every day they face the same soldiers, the same lines, the same questions, the same uncertainties."

"Like rats in a maze?"

"A not totally predictable maze. It robs them of their dignity. Such a pity."

Sounds like way more than a pity to me. Sounds outrageous.

"They are carrying lunch bags, not weapons. Every day, every day."

Khulood gently took Melody's hand as they walked away from the exit. Melody felt the heat of the sun on her back as she scanned the sea of yellow taxi cabs and stands selling cigarettes, sandwiches, tea, canned food, and coffee. She shook her head and sighed. "I just hope Yaz gets here." *This place is crazy. I know she's gonna be angry with me. BUT I NEED HER.*

She stared at the graffiti on the concrete wall that stretched in either direction. A giant scissors cut a dotted line. An enormous hand with a heart in its palm. FREE PALESTINE! Bits of trash, paper coffee cups, discarded wrappers, black plastic bags, piled at the base of the concrete wall. A small bird swooped over the rolls of barbed wire at the top. "Is this," she gestured, "like all around the city?"

"Yes dear, Bethlehem is completely surrounded. Like I said, it's a prison, except for the birds." She pointed to the little bird. "And the butterflies of course."

"How can people stand this?"

"They can't. Look at the graffiti." Khulood raised her eyebrows and nodded. "But what choice do we have?" She shrugged. "Now let's see if your friend is here."

Melody's phone pinged. She stared at the text from Yasmina.

My uncle Mahmoud has taxi, he is coming. He knows you have red hair.

Suddenly, she heard a high-pitched whistle. "Melodeee, over here!"

She turned to see an older man waving vigorously from a car window parked away from the taxis and the crowds. *Mahmoud? Thank god some-one's here.* Melody turned and looked at Khulood. Then she stopped. *This is crazy. She really looked out for me.* She felt the tears rising. *I trust her. And now…I'm losing her.*

Suddenly, she threw her arms around Khulood. A heavy lump grew in her throat. "Thank you, so much. You were sooo helpful," she choked. Melody clung to her.

Khulood patted her on the back, then held her shoulders and untangled their bodies. She looked into her eyes. "No problem. That's your friend?"

"Her uncle with a taxi."

"So, good. Don't worry. He will look out for you. Be happy. Take care dear, take care. Now, I need to get to work." She reached into her pocket and pressed another sesame candy into Melody's hand. "For the road, add sweetness to your journey. And if you have a problem, here's my number." She handed her a crumpled piece of paper. Melody smiled as Khulood waved at Mahmoud and then turned back to the taxis. Melody waved one last time at her new friend. She stuck the rumpled paper in her pocket and walked slowly toward Yasmina's uncle.

Chapter Seventeen

INNOCENT CHILD

"**Y**OU ARE MELODY? I AM MAHMOUD. You call me Uncle. Get in, get in. Welcome to Palestine." He folded the sleeves of his crisp gray shirt toward his elbows and opened the front passenger door, gesturing to her.

Melody hesitated. She stared at the long scar on his arm. *Get in a car with a strange man? Alone. Not my uncle. I don't know him. I don't even know where I'm going.* Aaron's warnings lit up her brain.

"I, I can't afford a taxi." She reached into her back pocket and pulled out her phone. "I need to text someone," she mumbled. She could feel the rapid drumming in her chest. Her brain was shouting. *Just leave. Walk away. What are you doing?*

"This is no problem." Mahmoud smiled. "Yasmina said you are family. I was driving nearby. Please, no charge. No worry."

"You talked to Yasmina?"

He pointed to his phone. "She just texted me."

Melody stared at the text. Alarm bells rang in her head. *Yaz sent him a message, but this is so…unnerving.* She flashed to Dov's pawing under her shirt, the soldier yelling at the girl to spread-eagle. *Why should I trust this guy? What if Aaron was right?* She looked around at the cars parked in a jumble, laborers with dirt-stained hands and men in sharply ironed shirts walking along the road, a donkey and cart loaded with large green melons. The donkey shook the flies off its face and squawked hoarsely, its nostrils wide. She scanned the mishmash of bodies and cars and animals. No one looked alarmed. No one even noticed her. Not even the donkey.

"Really, no problem, I will drive you to Hebron, to Yasmina's family house. She is like a daughter to me." Mahmoud smiled again. "Hot day." He wiped his brow with a white cotton handkerchief.

Melody took a deep breath. *Yaz said he would be here. Damn, he's old enough to be my father.* She glanced at his head of thick black curls, salted with gray. *And friendly. What are my options? Who can I rely on?* She swept her fingers over her bracelet, muttered, "Stick with me, Mom," and slid slowly onto the front passenger seat.

She plopped her backpack between her knees, keeping a tight hold on one of the straps. Just in case. A chain with a photo of Al Aqsa Mosque dangled from the mirror along with a photo of five kids, grinning for the camera. *Okay, he has kids. Teenagers.* The radio sang jangly Arabic music. She clicked on her seatbelt. *Hope he's not a lunatic driver.*

"So you come to see your friend?"

Melody nodded as Mahmoud pulled away from the checkpoint and headed down a narrow road dwarfed by the concrete wall. *I can always jump out if he's creepy. But then what?* Melody leaned her elbow on the edge of the window and played nervously with her nose ring.

"First time in Palestine?" Melody turned and nodded. She had to admit she liked the playful twinkle in his eyes and the way his ebony mustache wiggled when he spoke. But still.

"Ah! You are an innocent child. I will be your tour guide." He smiled. "My pleasure."

"I'm not a child." She sat up straight. *That is so annoying. Traveling alone, smoking weed. Dov and his creepy hands. That qualifies. Not. So. Innocent.*

"Did Yasmina tell you anything?"

Melody felt a shiver of fear and self-doubt. "No, not really." *What does he mean? What kind of anything? What was Yasmina hiding?*

"Let me show you the beauty in our homeland. This is a hard place. You will see. So, we are in Bethlehem, very important to the Christians, now here is the main street." He pointed in the direction of a large stone building with arches and turrets.

Okay, this could be…interesting. Just don't relax. She clutched her phone in her hand, rubbing its smooth surface, round and round, black fingernails against the red case. Melody looked out the window. The phone felt like a tiny anchor, a connection, an escape.

"Is that a castle or something?"

"Lovely, yes? Jacir Palace Hotel. It was built by a rich family, early 1900s. The British made it into a prison. Then it was a school. The Israeli army took it as a base in the First Intifada. Now it is a hotel." He shook his head and smiled. "Ah. Such a story."

Oh, this is going to be another history lesson. "Inti—what?" Melody tilted her head and looked at him.

"In-ti-fa-da. Arabic. Popular uprising."

"Intifada?"

"Yes. There have been two intifadas here, two times when we Palestinians tried to shake off the Israeli occupiers." He lit a cigarette. "Okay with you? I keep the window open."

Melody wrinkled her nose and opened her window a bit. She thought about the word uprising and the word terrorist. She thought about being trapped in a car with a strange man with a purple scar on his arm. *What would Aaron say? Or Malkah? Or my dad? He would just kill me.* Her knee jittered and she wrapped her arms around her chest, on alert, her curls bouncing in the wind from the partially opened window.

Mahmoud suddenly swung the taxi into a parking place next to a row of cabs. "One minute." As he hoisted himself out of the car leaving a trail of ash on the seat, Melody pondered her options. *If this is for real, then I'm okay. But why is he stopping? If I'm being kidnapped, then maybe I should jump out now, there are lots of people around. Would my dad even pay to get me back? I could run.* She reached into her pocket and felt Khulood's crumpled phone number. *I could call Yaz. I could...*

Before she could complete her next thought, Mahmoud returned, smiling, and gestured to Melody. Through the partially opened window he handed her a pita bread loaded with lamb and salad dripping with garlic sauce, wrapped in wax paper. "You like shawarma? I thought you might be hungry. And here, to drink." He handed her a bottle of Coke and a bunch of napkins. "You like French fries?"

"Thank you." Melody felt vaguely embarrassed. "How much?"

"Please, I welcome you to my homeland. Enjoy."

Melody suddenly felt very hungry as the fragrant smell filled the taxi. She bit into a French fry. *God, that's good. Does he think I'll trust him if he feeds me? Maybe it's like a bribe? But Yaz's mom is always feeding me. They like to feed people. I'm okay.*

"Thank you." She smiled and hungrily chomped into the shawarma as garlic sauce dribbled down her chin.

Mahmoud got into the car, sipping a small cup of strong Turkish coffee. "You want coffee too?" He lit another cigarette. "Excuse my cigarettes. I tell my passengers, I will stop smoking when the occupation ends." He laughed. "Too much stress."

"No, I...I'm only sixteen. I don't really drink coffee. And I don't smoke cigarettes either."

"Good, you are a smart girl." He pulled the taxi out onto the street. "See up the hill the stone buildings? That's Bethlehem University. That over there in front of us is the intersection of the Hebron Jerusalem Road, Bab Zqaq. So off we go."

Melody took another bite and relaxed into her seat.

"Bab Zqaq, there used to be a spring here. Drink your Coke, it's a hot day."

I guess this is The Official Tour. She thought about the Star of David under her shirt. *What would he think of that? What would Aaron think of this? I really need to talk with Yaz.* "How long to get there?"

"Maybe...one hour, maybe...even two hours, depending on the checkpoints."

Melody did a double take. *What, two hours? How could I expect Yaz to meet me? On short notice. I really don't know what I'm doing. Or where I'm going for that matter.* She took a deep breath and bit into another French fry.

Mahmoud pointed to an intersection. "This is Bayt Jala, a beautiful old town, Christian town."

Melody balanced her shawarma and fries in one hand and sipped her drink. *Christian?* She stared at the graceful buildings, porches bursting with flowers, trellises draped with blossoms, churches with pointy steeples and crosses. "Wow, what a view."

"Ah, you like the old stones, the geraniums and bougainvillea, so much beauty. But you will see, the scars of occupation are everywhere."

"Is that like a whole sheep or cow or something hanging on that hook?" *Gross.* She squirmed and looked cautiously at her half-eaten sandwich, staring at the fragments of meat and lettuce.

"This is a market area, yes, butchers, and vegetable stands. Everything grows in Palestine. So lovely. Praise God."

Melody gazed at the pyramids of watermelon and the boxes overflowing with peppers, cucumbers, and tomatoes. *Maybe I could be a vegetarian here...* She took another bite of shawarma. The houses got closer together. She noticed more trash on the street; two barefoot little boys kicked a scruffy soccer ball.

"This, my dear is Dheisheh Refugee Camp. 15,000 people live here, all crowded together, very poor. You know about refugee camps?"

Melody looked at the low concrete wall, cracked and broken down, and behind the wall, a blocky sign in Arabic and English, DHEISHEH CULTURAL CENTER. Two scraggly cats perched on the edge of the wall eyeing a big blue dumpster overflowing with garbage. She thought about history class back home, photos of skinny children in foreign countries waiting in line for a bowl of rice, swollen bellies, their heads too big for their starving bodies. *War. Drought. But here?* She shook her head no. A feral dog slunk by, ribs rippling under his skin. *Oh that poor dog.* Her brain flashed to Cheddar, his solid furry body. *Well fed.*

"During the 1948 war, the Arab/Israeli War, hundreds of thousands of Palestinians were driven out of their homes and became refugees. Now we have many generations living in camps, though some like me live in towns and cities."

"Are you a refugee?"

"My family is from the ancient village of Bayt Jibrin, over 2,000 years old, so beautiful, but destroyed in '48. It's now a tourist place, a national park and Jewish town called Beit Govrin. In Israel.

"So you live in a refugee camp?"

"No. Now we live in Hebron, the city of Hebron."

"Oh," Melody nodded, licking her fingers and wiping her hands. *I wonder if Yasmina is a refugee?*

"Every Palestinian has a story of exile."

As the taxi sped along Mahmoud added, "This is the area of Solomon's pools, maybe 2,000 years old. And here are factories, mostly granite. Did you know that Hebron is famous for its stone quarries and glass blowing?"

"I'm sorry. I really don't know anything about Hebron." She watched the large factories fade away as the land became more rural, rolling hills, knots of sheep and solitary goats munching the low vegetation. The taxi drove up a small hill toward a roundabout when Mahmoud hit the brakes. "Ah, a flying checkpoint."

Chapter Eighteen

GET OUT OF THE CAR

ELODY STARED AHEAD AT THE ROW OF BACKED-UP cars and a battered truck with two sheep in the cargo bed. She could hear their plaintive bleating and smelled the smoky exhaust of idling vehicles. The guy in the truck kept leaning out of the window, staring at the sheep. Melody sensed his worry. *Probably the heat. No water. Can sheep pass out?* She noticed that Israeli soldiers had parked a jeep across the road and were stopping each driver, then waving them through.

Melody and Mahmoud sat in silence. He turned off the radio. An ambulance pulled up behind them.

What the fuck is this?

Mahmoud lit another cigarette. "Don't worry, happens all the time. We're fine."

Don't worry? I don't even know what to worry about. I could get lung cancer by the time we get there. "What are they looking for?" She craned her head sidewise to better see the soldiers, their olive green uniforms, heavy brown boots, guns strapped over their shoulders.

"You never know. Sometimes I think they just want to remind us who's in charge."

"In charge? Are we in Israel or not?"

"This is occupied territory, Palestine, but the Israeli army rules. It's also where the road turns off for the settlers. Get out your passport."

Melody scrambled to pull up her backpack with one hand and dug for her passport. She gripped it firmly. *This should protect me, right?* She took her last bite of shawarma and crumpled the paper into a ball and held it tightly in her other fist.

The taxi inched forward, followed by the ambulance, five cars, a white van with blue UN lettering, and a truck filled with tomatoes. Finally a soldier wearing an enormous helmet, a rifle on his back, bent toward the open car window. "Papers?"

Mahmoud handed him his green ID and driver's license, and the soldier straightened up. The car was silent. Melody bit her lip and stared straight ahead. She tapped a finger on her passport. *Guns, guns, and more guns. These guys scare me.*

The soldier handed the ID back and pointed at Melody. "American? Passport?"

She handed it to Mahmoud who handed it to the soldier.

He opened it, thumbed through the pages and handed it back, waving his arm. "Okay. Yalla, go."

Mahmoud turned the ignition and the car moved forward. Melody realized she had been holding her breath. Mahmoud glanced at her. "You okay? This is occupation. The Israelis control so much, but we live our lives. I want you to understand that. And you are safe with me."

"What's a settler?"

"Ah, you are an innocent child, my dear."

"I'm actually sixteen going on…"

"Yes, I have a fifteen-year-old daughter. She is a lot like you, adventuresome, full of questions, but not a big understanding of the world. She was so happy to see her cousin, Yasmina. I mean, they talk on the phone and Facebook, do that Twittering/Instagram thing, stuff I don't understand. She really wants to visit America."

"It's really different at home." Melody felt a sudden yearning for the quiet tree-lined streets, the gentle flow of traffic, the rush of students between classes. "What's her name? Does she speak English?"

"Noura. She will like you. She will practice her English on you."

Melody smiled for the first time, put her phone down on her lap, and slipped her passport back into her bag.

"About settlers. There was a war in 1967, and the Israeli army took over this part of Palestine from Jordan. They took the West Bank, as well as East Jerusalem and…"

"I've been in Jerusalem, the Old City. Is that east or west?"

"The Old City? Part of East Jerusalem, Arab Jerusalem. That's when Israel also took Gaza from Egypt. And then Jewish people, Israelis, but also people from your America." He wagged his nicotine-stained finger at her and raised his eyebrows. "They started settling, building towns and cities on Palestinian land."

"Those are the settlers?"

"Yes. All illegal colonies. Even in the middle of the Arab city of Hebron, my home." He swept his hand across the windshield. "And we Palestinians, we suffer even more." He picked up his lighter and sucked deeply on his cigarette.

Melody stared out the window as the taxi headed south on Route 60, fields and terraced olive orchards raced by. She thought about Aaron's cousin living near Hebron. *Is he a settler? He's gotta be.* She shifted her weight in the seat, her back ached. *Too much sitting. Too much tension. Too much really bad stuff.*

Mahmoud pulled the taxi to the side of the road. He pointed at some small caravans in the distance and then large clusters of multi-story white apartments climbing up the hill. "Gush Etzion."

Melody pointed at the huge cranes towering over the buildings. "Jewish settlement? That's like a big city."

Mahmoud nodded. "On a construction frenzy. Financed by Americans." He pulled the taxi back onto the road. "See here, now Gush Etzion is on both sides of the road. So dangerous, so dangerous."

"Why?"

"Ah, so imagine there is a war. The enemy is on both sides of the highway. And we are running the gauntlet. You know that word? Gauntlet? Like in the movies?"

Melody nodded slowly. *What is he talking about?* They headed through a roundabout, and suddenly Melody gaped at the four guard posts, draped with camouflage netting, soldiers holding large guns, fingers on the triggers. An enormous Israeli flag hung listlessly from a pole. On both sides of the highway, bus stops were clustered with people, the women in longish skirts.

"Got it." Melody stared at the women, most wearing scarves covering their hair. "Are those wigs?"

Mahmoud nodded. "Orthodox Jews. Israeli Jews. The men have beards and skull caps."

She recognized the look of the boys in black pants and white shirts and the off-duty soldiers carrying automatic rifles. *Just like Jerusalem.*

"Settlers?" Melody asked.

Mahmoud nodded and slowed down. "This is a tense intersection. We call it the intersection of death."

Great. Melody reached for her passport again, anxiously running her finger over the embossed gold letters, United States of America, glowing against the deep blue background.

As she opened her passport, an Israeli soldier stepped into the road and pointed at the taxi. Melody looked up. Mahmoud stopped.

The soldier pointed at Mahmoud and Melody. "Papers. Get out of the car."

Mahmoud looked at Melody. "Stay calm and do what the soldiers say. No questions. No arguing. Keep your hands out of your pockets."

Fuck. This whole place is a war zone. "Okay, okay," she said quietly. Melody handed Mahmoud her passport. Her hand shook as she opened the door and stood stiffly next to the taxi. Mahmoud came around and stood next to her. The unrelenting sun made the place feel like a hot griddle.

I'm gonna' melt out here, if I don't die of fright first. What insanity. She stared at the soldier's peach fuzz of a mustache. A group of little boys approached them, pointing and chattering in Hebrew. *Fuck, fuck, fuck.*

The soldier returned the papers and yelled, "Open your trunk!" Mahmoud slowly walked to the back of the taxi and unlocked the trunk. He stood quietly, staring at the ground, his hands dangling by his sides. Two soldiers started rifling through his things, bottles of water, bags of rice, a tire repair kit. The little boys walked closer. Suddenly, one of them threw a piece of rotting fruit at Melody and hit her in the back of the leg. She turned as another splatted on her tee shirt.

"Those little punks just hit me. Why did they do that?" Melody stifled an urge to run after them, grab them and shake them.

Mahmoud glared at her and raised his eyebrows. Melody slapped her hand over her mouth. *Now I'm definitely gonna die.* Her pulse throbbed wildly and a mix of rage and terror shook her body. She grabbed her silver bracelet as tears surged. She wiped her eyes quickly and moved closer to Mahmoud. The little boys giggled and ran back to the bus stop, hiding behind their mothers. Melody flicked the dripping mess off her shirt and stuffed her hands in her pockets. She rubbed one leg against the other as the wet fruit dripped into her sock. *Just hold together and shut up. Shut up! Why doesn't anyone stop those awful kids? Oh, god, I've got to get my hands out of my pockets.*

The soldiers slammed the trunk down and pointed at Mahmoud. "Pull up your shirt. Turn around. Slowly."

Melody held her breath. *Holy shit.* Her whole body froze. *What are they gonna do to him? Or to me?* She could feel a slow river of sweat wandering down her back. She felt ambushed by the boys, by the soldiers, by her out-of-control life. And here she was stuck at some god-forsaken checkpoint with some teenage soldier pointing his gun at her. *I'm so not ready for this.*

Mahmoud exhaled deliberately, pulled up his shirt, and turned slowly around in front of the soldier.

Melody looked at him, his pale belly thick with curly black hair, and recognized his look of quiet resignation. Suddenly she understood Khulood's "daily humiliation" comment. She felt a flush of embarrassment, watching the young soldier boss Mahmoud around. *I bet that soldier's the same age as his kids.*

The soldier gestured for them to get back in the car.

Chapter Nineteen

TOO MUCH AWFULNESS

MELODY LEAPED INTO HER SEAT AND LOCKED THE DOOR. She stared straight ahead, her fingers pressed against her passport. *Just get moving, GET MOVING. Start the car.* Her pulse pounded and she felt that edge of panic returning. *Just start the fucking car.* The edges of her vision began tunneling into blackness. *Okay, count and breathe.* She tapped her fingers nervously on her knee. *I'm falling apart.*

Mahmoud inserted the key and the engine choked and rumbled as the taxi moved forward. He clenched his jaw on and off, the muscles in his face tightening and rippling.

Melody's body shuddered and this deep sob rattled her chest. She felt so abandoned, by her dead mother, her absent father. Did Yasmina even care? Aaron was useless. "I'm sorry, I'm sorry," she blubbered as more tears began to flow. "Why did they do that to you?" A torrent of pent-up grief, fear, and confusion invaded her and spilled over the walls of her emotional fortress.

"There's just too much awfulness. Everywhere. How can you stand it?" She curled into her seat and hung her head, rubbing her forehead as tears dripped down her cheeks, enveloped by that old, familiar feeling, the empty unfairness of her life, of her whole shitty world. "My mom is dead," she said suddenly. Melody gyrated toward the window, her guts twisting. A shockwave of despair convulsed her mind.

Mahmoud nodded.

"Cancer," she whispered hoarsely.

Mahmoud nodded again.

"And my dad, you don't know him. He's so useless. All he cares about is work. I'm like a fucking orphan, sorry," she shuddered. "He flies me here, like this is some kind of treat, and says go explore, like I'm one of his PhD students on an archeology dig." She threw her hands up. "I'm just a kid." Melody stared out the window, feeling like a giant dam was bursting inside of her and she couldn't control the flood. "I'm drowning."

"I see."

"I was visiting my cousin in Tel Aviv and this awful thing happened. And that big checkpoint in Bethlehem." Melody spluttered, caught herself, and took a deep breath. "I don't know what to do. How do I deal with all this?" She turned toward Mahmoud. "How do you deal with this? Should I even be telling you this?"

Mahmoud reached into his pocket and handed her a folded handkerchief. She shook it open, blew her nose loudly and dabbed her eyes, smearing her mascara beyond repair.

"I mean, and then you show me the refugee camps and the barefoot little kids, even their soccer ball was ragged. And those awful settler boys. I, I just don't know what to think. Or do." Melody wept uncontrollably, the weight of her grief and confusion smothering her. "I thought Yasmina could help me, she's like my big sister. I'm, I'm so alone." Mascara tears mingled with her freckles. She wiped her face, the handkerchief streaked a charcoal black. "Oh god, I must look awful." She blew her nose again.

Mahmoud pulled to the side of the road, stopped the car, and looked at Melody as a green valley layered with rows of twisting grapevines spread before them. He lit another cigarette. "Welcome to Palestine." He spit out a bit of tobacco.

Melody looked at him, eyebrows bunching on her forehead. "Have you ever fired a gun?" He blew a cloud of smoke toward the open window and smiled. "My dear, I have never touched a weapon."

"Never?"

"I was a teacher, but no jobs, no salary, so now I drive a taxi." He nodded as Melody gazed at his face, the tiredness in his eyes, the downward turn of his lower lip, the fierceness in the way he held his head. "That soldier boy, he had to prove his manhood, what a big tough guy he is. And he thinks I am the enemy, the Arab enemy. There is no justice in life, only stubbornness and the resolve to survive."

They sat in silence as Melody tried to calm her rattled nerves and wrap her brain around her sorrow, her confusion. *Soldiers. Taunting boys. Humiliation. Survival.* She took a tissue from her pack and dabbed her stained tee shirt. Mahmoud reached for the radio when Melody's phone pinged.

Chapter Twenty

INJUSTICE TOUR

S HE LOOKED DOWN AT THE MESSAGE. *Aaron. Oh, yeah, back on planet Vermont. Still happening.*

Can't stop thinking about u. Can't sleep. Why didn't u answer? Where are u?"

Melody sighed. *How do I explain this?*

Sorry. Taxi to Hebron. Don't worry. ☺

Like in Judea and Samaria? Other side of the fence????

NOT A FENCE. I came thru Bethlehem checkpoint *** huge concrete prison wall*** 🏚

U don't know what ur doing. Ur gonna get killed!!!!! 😨, 😟

Melody pictured him bent over his phone, typing wildly, in a panic, hair exploding. A minivan scooted around the taxi. Grapevines lined the road and a herd of goats trotted along the highway.

It's not really how you think. Met some really nice people.

Exception to the rule.

Nice, except Israeli soldiers.

They're protecting u!!!! 🖼

Kids threw stuff at me!!!!

What do u expect from Arabs!

Jewish kids.

U sure????

Of course I'm sure.

Melody leaned back in her seat and stared up at the torn fabric on the ceiling. *This is so confusing. It's not so us and them. He doesn't get it.*

Will text you when I get to Yaz, send you some photos. Can't talk now. DON'T WORRY!!! She searched for an emoji. Hungry kid? Olive tree? Donkey?

Don't do anything stupid. OK? WORRIED. Praying for you.

Don't bother. She closed her eyes and tried to steady herself. *Settlements, refugee camps, poverty. Obnoxious little boys throwing stuff and no one stops them. What kind of world is this? How can I explain this to him?*

Mahmoud started the ignition and rolled onto the highway. "Look around, dear." He pointed. "See those Palestinian villages, tucked into the hills. The ones with the black water tanks on their roofs. Water comes and goes, controlled by the Israelis, of course. So we store it on our roofs."

Back on the tour of injustice. Melody sighed. She took out her phone and snagged a photo.

"See, the villages are surrounded by fields. The Jewish settlements are perched on the tops of hills like military fortifications, circles of red roofs surrounded by walls and barbed wire. See over there."

Click.

She spotted a jumble of one-story buildings, crammed together, punctuated by a tall thin minaret. Large concrete blocks and wire fencing along the road. A heavy yellow gate. Behind this lay a stunning valley. "Refugee camp?" More photos. Click. Click. Mahmoud slowed down. Click. "For my friend Aaron."

Mahmoud smiled and nodded. "Yes, Arroub Refugee Camp. You are such a smart girl. Already you are understanding my beloved landscape. You hungry? Thirsty?" He reached for a chocolate wafer bar lying under the dashboard.

Melody shook her head. "No thanks." She stared at the bar... "That's chocolate?" She smiled. "Can I change my mind? I could use some candy." She reached for the bar. "Stress relief, like your cigarettes." Her face darkened. "What's with that tower and the soldiers over there?"

"Always big problems. Big problems."

More trouble? Melody held her breath as they drove past. *Are those blindfolded kids? OMG!* She stared at a cluster of teenage boys sitting cross-legged on the ground, heads tilted up, eyes blindfolded, their hands cuffed behind their backs, sweating in the sun. She snapped another photo. *Definitely for Aaron.*

"Be careful with your photos," Mahmoud interrupted. "Military. Be quick."

She dropped her phone below the window. Suddenly, it rang, piercing the silence. She jumped. *My dad said not to make calls here. Shit, it is my dad.*

Ring, ring, ring.

"You answer it?" Mahmoud asked.

"Hello, Dad." Melody's voice sounded small.

"Where are you and what the hell are you doing, young lady? I was presenting at the conference. I just saw your text."

"I'm, I'm in a taxi, Dad."

"Where are you?"

Melody turned to Mahmoud. "Where are we?"

"Near Bayt Ummar," Mahmoud replied.

"We're near Bayt Ummar."

"Where the hell is that? We???"

"In a taxi. I'm going to Hebron, see Yaz."

"You can't do that!"

"What do you care? I'm doing it."

Her father fell silent. Melody was afraid he could hear her heart thumping. She twirled her silver bracelet. *Just-leave-me-a-lone.*

"Mel, listen honey. Does the driver speak English? Let me talk to him. You need to come back."

"I'm not coming back."

"Mel, give me a chance here." She hung up and stared out at the terraced rolling hills. *Forget about him.* She saw a cluster of houses in the distance with black water tanks on their roofs. Palestinian.

Mahmoud glanced at her with a questioning look. He slowed the taxi down. Stopped. Stared at her. "Your father? You're running away?"

Melody took a deep breath and shook her head. "I really can take care of myself. I don't need two dad's telling me what to do. Thank you very much." She crossed her arms across her chest and glared out the window, suddenly focused on a scrawny grey cat followed by two skinny kittens slinking along the road, hollow-eyed. Anxiety shimmered at the edges of her defiance. *My dad has no idea what happened to me. What's happening all around me. Just look out the window. Does he even know about this place? Those kittens are starving.*

The phone rang again.

"Mel, honey…."

Melody handed her phone to Mahmoud. Her demons were screaming *what the hell are you doing???* But before she totally crumpled inside, she said, "It's my dad. Tell him I'm not coming back." Her eyes reddened and her tears flooded, like a dam ready to burst.

A wisp of smoke curled from the cigarette dangling from Mahmoud's lips. Melody saw a concerned father look in his eyes. Damn.

"Hello, sir. Mahmoud Khdour here."

Chapter Twenty-One

FATHERS

"**G**OOD TO MEET YOU, sir."

"Phillip, yes, she is in the car, sir."

"Yes, yes, I understand."

Melody glared at him. *Whose side are you on?*

"Children, yes, yes…I have five of my own. Of course."

She leaned forward, trying to hear her father's voice. *Was he shouting or…crying?*

"Of course, you don't want to lose her."

Mahmoud leaned his shoulder against the phone and juggled another cigarette.

Melody rolled her window down all the way and fanned the hot air with her hand.

"Yes sir, I appreciate what you are saying. I lost a son of my own. It was a long time ago, but still…"

"Your wife, I'm so sorry."

"Yes, yes, Yasmina's uncle's house. No problem."

"His name? Kareem Khdour."

"Yes, his wife's name is Sara."

"Yes, Arabic, like Sarah in English."

"South of the city, a suburb. Nice house. I promise you, she will be fine."

"Of course. Not where all the trouble is."

Melody leaned her head into her hands and slumped onto the dashboard. *Will they ever stop talking? What is going on?* She felt her nose ring pressing against her palm, making little half-moons. *Just strangle me already.*

"Yes of course, I promise."

"I will not let her out of my sight."

Melody sat up and glared at him.

"Right, I will have him call you. This is your cell?"

"Goodbye Phillip."

Mahmoud dropped the phone into his lap. He turned and winked slyly at her.

"Well?"

"Young lady. Your father is very worried about you. In fact he is quite angry with you."

Duh, what else is new? I hate him.

"But he knows how close Yasmina is to you. He has agreed..."

"Agreed?"

"He has agreed that you may stay with them for three days. Mr. Khdour needs to call him when you arrive. He will come to Hebron to meet her family and take you back to Jerusalem."

"Really?"

"Really."

Melody stretched out her long legs and pushed back against the seat. She turned toward Mahmoud, the rage and the fear emptied out of her body, her eyes watery. A drip of black mascara gathered on her eyelid. "Thank you." *I don't want to cry now.* She wiped her eye with the back of her hand creating a dark smudge on her cheek.

"Then it is settled. Wipe your face. Shall we get back to the tour?"

"Wait, you said you lost a son?"

Mahmoud turned the key and swung the car onto the highway. He stared ahead, silent. His hands tightly gripped the steering wheel, knuckles pale. The road wound to the right and then up a hill. She saw houses, stores, a mechanic's shop crowded with parked cars. Mahmoud nodded at the looming gray guard tower, military jeeps, and huddle of Israeli soldiers. Melody stared at the yellow gate, the people and taxis crowded at the entrance to a village, the flat-roofed stone houses meandering up the hill. "Bayt Ummar."

"Palestinian village?"

Mahmoud nodded. "Occupied Palestinian village..." He turned the radio on.

They continued driving over undulating hills surrounded by terraced olive trees, stretches of grapevines, rows of almond trees. Melody fidgeted with her bracelet. *Did I say the wrong thing? I'm so nosy. A son? Dead?*

In the jangle of music, she was flooded with death memories, the hospital visits, the harsh disinfectant smell of the room, days staring at the drip, drip of IVs, her mother's sallow, sunken cheeks. The scent of lemon soap and decaying flesh. *Everyone said she was dying, but still...I always hoped. I never believed them. Dying. It's so... forever.* She gripped her hands together, her black fingernails cutting into her skin. Mahmoud coughed and switched the radio off. The guttural sound followed by silence pulled Melody into the present. She turned toward him.

"Young lady, I am a father too. A father loves his children even when he does not know how to tell them." He looked directly at her. "My young boy, Ibrahim, he was killed by an Israeli soldier. If he had lived, he would be 16 now, just like you."

Melody's eyes jolted wide open. "I'm so, so, sorry." She exhaled loudly and put her hands together as if she were praying. "Yasmina told me about her cousin. I, I didn't know he was your son."

"Yes, my beloved little man." He lit a cigarette and smoked in silence. Melody stared out the window at a young boy riding bareback on a gray horse, hooves kicking up dust, his bottom bouncing up and down, his clothes dappled with fine sand. *Did he look like that boy? Ride a horse? Feel the sweltering sun on his back?*

A thought kept circling in her mind. *So much of my life sucks, but I am alive. I am safe where I live. No one is trying to kill anyone. I am not poor. I wasn't raped. What right do I have to complain?*

Chapter Twenty-Two

TIRED AND ANGRY

MAHMOUD BENT FORWARD AND LIT ANOTHER cigarette, ash littering his shirt. "Enough of this talk." He dropped the lighter on the dashboard. "We are coming through Halhoul, north Hebron," he pointed. "We call Hebron, Al Khalil in Arabic."

Melody looked down the busy street, clothing stores with big windows, a shoe store, electronics, jewelry, a bakery with shelves of delicacies, several layers of apartments above. It all looked pretty...normal.

"Ah, see here is the Hebron Glass and Ceramics Factory. The city is known for glass blowing. Very beautiful. You know glass blowing?"

As Mahmoud slowed down, Melody stared at the factory decorated with swirly tiles and Arabic lettering. She was relieved they'd stopped talking about dead people. "Yeah, sort of. So this is Hebron?"

"Yes." He turned right. "And now we are on Ein Sarah Street. You want ice cream?"

"No thank you." She was starting to feel anxious about seeing Yasmina. A wave of nausea, a sour taste at the back of her throat. *Why didn't she want me to come? Are we still friends? What am I even doing here?* She rubbed her tattoo with her thumb, first the rose and then the leaves, bumping over her scars, and back to the rose. She traced her finger over the M-O-M.

"Look here. Big commercial center, restaurants, fancy shops. Good place to buy shoes, nice clothes. You like shoes? We just head through this circle, Manara Circle. Now mostly doctors' offices and clinics. You see..."

"Wait a minute." Melody hung her head and then peeked at him sideways. "Sorry. Can I ask you a personal question?"

Mahmoud nodded.

"Tell me what's happening. Yasmina didn't want me to come." *And Aaron sure as hell didn't want to me visit.*

"Ah, let me explain." He raised one eyebrow. "Hebron is a holy city for Muslims and Jews. You know Bible stories?"

"Not really." *Doesn't anyone around here live in the twenty-first century?*

"Hebron is where Ibrahim, you call him Abraham, the father of Islam, Judaism, and Christianity, along with his wife Sarah were buried. And some of their descendants. In the Al-Ibrahimi Mosque. You call it the Cave of Machpelah. How do you say in English?"

Melody looked blank.

"Ah, Cave of the Patriarchs. So now there is a mosque and a synagogue on the same site and frequent fights about who prays when and where. But the Israelis, of course, are always in charge." He honked his horn and waved at an old man sitting, drinking coffee. "Hello my friend," he yelled. "There is even a Moslem entrance for Palestinians and tourists who are not Jewish and a Jewish entrance for Israeli Jews and tourists who are not Muslim."

"Look, I don't mean to interrupt, but what does this have to do with Yasmina? Like today. Like now. Is she okay?"

"My dear, don't worry, your Yasmina is fine. But history does matter. Even ancient history."

Melody groaned. "My dad always says that."

"This city was a mostly Muslim city for centuries, Muslims living peacefully with a small group of Jews, until Jewish settlers arrived and claimed the city for themselves. There have been riots and massacres. Between Muslims and Jews. And before that, against the British."

Melody felt like her brain was going to melt into a puddle, right in the taxi. Possibly splattering on the floor. Possibly making a very big mess. She leaned back in her seat and stared out the window.

"In 1968, on the outskirts of the city, a small group of settlers established Kiryat Arba…"

Melody's head shot up. "Wait a minute, what was that called?"

"The settlement? Kiryat Arba, very bad people, very violent."

Oh man, that's where Aaron's cousin lives? That's his source of information? She fidgeted with her bracelet.

"Then in 1979…are you listening?"

"My friend's cousin lives in Kiryat Arba."

"Then you need to listen to me. Very carefully."

Melody's eyes widened and she turned her whole body toward Mahmoud.

"Good. In 1979, a small group of settlers from Kiryat Arba entered the center of Hebron, the old city, and began establishing Israeli settlements there."

"Jewish settlements?"

"Very religious, aggressive, armed Jewish settlers, from Israel, many originally from the US. Hardliners. Fanatics. They terrorized us. And they still do."

"Terrorized? You?" She looked down at the scar on his arm and scanned his face. *Sounds like the fucking Ku Klux Klan.*

"In the old quarters of the city, there are checkpoints everywhere. Streets where we Palestinians are not allowed to drive or walk, even if our house, our front door, is on that street."

"But, but…how do you get out of your house?"

"We go out backdoors, backyards; some people use ladders and go roof to roof."

"That's nuts! That's so unfair, almost like, like segregation in my country. Big time." Her US history class popped into her brain. *Montgomery, Alabama. Red lining in the north. White people attacking Black people.*

"You see this scar?"

Melody nodded.

"A settler attacked me with the barrel of his gun. He and his buddies beat me hard, cut up my arm."

"Why?" *I bet Aaron's cousin doesn't tell him this kind of stuff. Not very holy behavior if you ask me.*

"I was harvesting my olives, on land my wife's family has owned for centuries, and the settlers claimed that land, forged documents and all. And the Israeli soldiers who roam the city," he threw up his hands, then gripped the wheel. "All they do is protect the settlers, against us. They use bullets, teargas, skunk water."

"Skunk what?" Melody thought about her cousin Daniel. *He's an Israeli soldier. Stationed in Hebron.*

"My dear, it's a very putrid liquid the soldiers spray and it sticks to your clothes, your skin, makes you vomit. It's like a mix of…feces, stinky gas, and…" He thought a moment. "A decomposing donkey. It's horrible."

Melody could barely imagine the smell of a decomposing donkey or a decomposing anything for that matter. The thought of it made her gag.

There was once a stinky rat that died in her wall and that was awful for days. But a stinking donkey?

She put her hand over face. Her pulse jolted at the idea of fanatical settlers, angry soldiers, wounded Palestinians, bullets. What had she gotten herself into?

"Is Yasmina's family safe? You sure Yasmina's safe?" She bit her lip and looked at Mahmoud. "Did something bad happen to Yasmina? Please tell me."

"Two weeks ago, several Palestinian children were attacked by settlers on the way to school, and one, a fifteen-year-old girl, was killed, shot dead. It's not clear if it was from a Jewish soldier or a settler, but it doesn't matter." He shook his head. "An innocent child, with a backpack full of books and school reports, was left to bleed to death in the street."

"Holy shit, I mean…" Melody searched for a word. "Oh no. That's terrible."

"So everyone's angry, fed up. During the day, there have been protests…"

"Wow. Like the Black Lives Matter protests in the States?"

Mahmoud nodded. "The marches end with the Israeli soldiers shooting teargas, bullets…"

"Like the police at home…"

"And sometimes skunk water. As night comes, more young men gather in the streets, throwing stones at soldiers and jeeps, burning tires. Calling for justice and an end to this occupation and the killing of innocent children."

"Tell me, are you sure Yasmina didn't get hurt?"

Mahmoud nodded reassuringly. "Did you know that Palestinian protests are illegal under occupation? Even waving the Palestinian flag is forbidden. A few days ago, Yasmina's uncle, Mr. Kareem Khdour, was out looking for his son Abdallah, he was so worried. The young man is not a stone thrower. He believes in marching, chanting, but resistance comes in many forms and anyone can get hurt. Mr. Kareem was hit in the head with a tear gas canister, shot directly at him, knocked unconscious."

Melody gasped. *Wait 'til I tell Aaron about this.*

"His leg was blasted with a bullet, the bone fragmented. He was in the hospital for days. He's home now, recovering. He was probably targeted because he is a journalist."

"Oh my gosh." Melody slapped her hand across her face. "I'm so sorry he was injured. So Yasmina is not hurt?"

Mahmoud shook his head gently. "Your friend has no physical injuries, but the family is hurting. There have been, of course, other injuries in the past, there was my son." He slid a cigarette into his mouth and turned toward her. "We are tired and we are very angry."

Mahmoud adjusted his glasses and continued. "In 1994 a Jewish doctor, American..." He looked directly at Melody and repeated, "American, massacred 29 Muslims and injured 200 Palestinians who were praying at the mosque. Obviously, there were protests and then more killings. What do you think the Israelis did?"

Melody shrugged her shoulders. She was paying close attention now, but she had no idea. Everything seemed kind of crazy, upside down.

"Did they put the Jews under curfew and protect the Muslims who were attacked?"

Melody exhaled slowly. "I get it. They protected the Jews."

"Exactly. They put a curfew on the Palestinians, permanently closed Arab businesses in the heart of the city, Tel Rumeida, and in the end, closed Shuhada Street, the major commercial center, forever." Mahmoud lit his cigarette, his hand shaking slightly as he grasped the lighter. "And then they divided the city into the Jewish-controlled part, H2, and the Muslim-controlled part. H1. Now we have 200,000 Palestinians and 1,000 Israeli settlers all living here, the settlers protected by 2,000 heavily armed Israeli soldiers. Even in H1 there are two Israeli military bases."

"That's so not fair."

Mahmoud nodded vigorously. "That policy crushed us economically and crushed our souls." He pulled out a handkerchief, blew his nose, and wiped his eyes.

Crying? Melody looked at his face closely.

"And it means we are constantly in danger from these settlers. You can't imagine. And protesting ends in arrest or worse."

Melody thought about Aaron. She thought about taking pictures in Hebron, documenting, showing him what she was seeing and hearing. *He is a good person but he just doesn't know. Especially if he is listening to his cousin.* She thought about changing his mind. "I want to see. Can you show me? I need to explain this to my friend back home. And to myself."

Mahmoud crossed several lanes of traffic and pulled the taxi over to the sidewalk. A cluster of red, yellow and blue umbrellas shielded a fruit stand piled with pomegranates and bananas from the hot sun. Men and women hustled along the street, chattering, going in and out of shops.

"You want me to show you Tel Rumeida and Shuhada Street?"

"Yes, yes, show me." Melody's heart pounded in her temples.

"Okay, but we must be very careful. And you must listen to me. Same rules. Don't argue. There are a lot of crazy soldiers here. And settlers." He turned off the road and soon pulled the car to the curb, parking about ten feet away from a large concrete block, stenciled in thick black letters: END APARTHIED NOW!!! OPEN SHUHADA STREET.

Chapter Twenty-Three

SHUHADA STREET

MELODY WALKED PAST THE CONCRETE BLOCKS, her heart thudding, a quiet fierceness growing inside of her. To the right she spotted a beige caravan with a metal detector, surrounded by concrete blocks, three Israeli soldiers chatting, their hands on their rifles, a cluster of women in hijabs and ankle length abayas, kids squirming, waiting. In front of her she saw a street littered with tear gas and broken bottles.

She turned to Mahmoud and nodded toward the caravan.

"Israeli checkpoint. Let's go left, down this side street to the main road."

As they walked, Melody looked down one winding passage and saw a Palestinian man washing his car. On another street, a loud honking and a car decorated with flowers and streamers. She heard a radio blasting lively music, a crowd of men singing along, laughing, arms over each other's shoulders. Mahmoud grinned, "Wedding party. You see, life goes on. We still fall in love."

"That's good." Melody blushed, embarrassed. *Of course people fall in love here. What was I thinking? Life does go on.* They walked slowly past old stone buildings, stores with clothes hanging out on the street, the fragrance of a spice shop drifting in the air, past butcher shops, restaurants, shops with burlap bags of nuts and candy, cheap gadgets from China. She felt the scorch of sun on her face. A little boy ran up to her, pulled on her backpack, peddling sticks of chewing gum. "Please lady, please."

Mahmoud handed him a few shekels and shooed him away with a pat on his shoulder. "There is so much poverty. Some of the families are desperate. They see you and think rich American."

Hardly. Melody thought about her home, all the things she took for granted. She wasn't rich rich, but still. Compared to some people here...

She wished she had bought the gum. As they continued walking, more shops were closed, their green metal gates locked.

Melody gasped. She took out her phone and clicked: DEATH TO ARABS! spray-painted across a shop gate, other doors marked with Jewish Stars of David. Click. Click.

"Be discrete," Mahmoud warned. "Look here." He pointed up at a row of apartment buildings, their windows encased in metal cages. A child waved at her from the window through the mesh. Melody smiled and waved back.

Click. "Why?" asked Melody

Mahmoud said quietly, "Palestinian homes. To protect against the settlers. They throw rocks at us, so we cover the windows with wire mesh."

"Rocks?" *Holy fuck.* She stared at a menacing grey Israeli watch tower. Click.

"Be very careful. You see that gate? Behind it is a Yeshiva, a Jewish school."

She gaped at the stone building, the rows of arched windows, the string of Israeli flags, the Star of David embedded in the stone.

"It used to be a high school for boys in the 1960s. The Israelis built several stories above the original building."

A soldier in front of the building scanned her suspiciously from afar. She stared up at a nearby watchtower covered in camouflage mesh, soldiers' heads visible at the top. Chatter in Hebrew and laughter. *Are they pointing at me?* Goosebumps erupted on her arms like a private alarm system.

As they kept walking, the quiet market bustle turned to deadly silence. "This is Tel Rumeida on Shehudah Street."

Melody's chest tightened, seized by a wave of anxiety. She took out her phone again and started taking pictures. Of everything. Her camera felt like a shield and a sword. The old market street was deserted, a row of shops all closed, their green doors welded shut, rusted green awnings hanging above the entries like tombstones. A ghost town. She walked up to one shop door and stared at the graffiti, another spray-painted Star of David. This reminded her of something, something from history class back home. *Shit. Like Nazi Germany only backwards.* Click. She felt her necklace burning into her skin. At another door, she froze: GAS THE ARABS, in thick black spray paint. Click, click.

"Be careful. Soldiers," Mahmoud touched her arm as a cluster of heavily armed young men in olive green uniforms, heavy boots thumping on the stone, appeared around the corner. A young man wearing a kippah jogged by. "There are three Israeli settlements on or near this street. Their residents can walk or drive anywhere. We can't." They continued quietly through stone arches, tangles of electrical wire, tattered awnings. Melody photographed a spray-painted THIS IS PALESTINE IN MY HEART, with an arrow pointing upward. Plastic bags and trash cluttered the borders of the street, layered up against old stone buildings and more closed shops.

A crowd of settler girls giggled and chattered in Hebrew as they headed up the road. They stared at Melody, unsure of who she was. Melody smiled nervously. A woman in a long grey abaya and hijab hustled by on the other side of the road, avoiding eye contact with anyone.

A stray cat meowed loudly as Melody looked at the broken windows and graffiti-stained walls. More black spray-painted Stars of David on shuttered shops. An Israeli army jeep sped down the street. Israeli flags fluttered from some of the houses. They passed a cross street completely blocked off by a tall concrete wall, guard towers and cameras everywhere. Soldiers peered over rooftops or crowded around concrete and metal checkpoints, joking, smoking, checking IDs. Women and children of all ages huddled in front of turnstiles and metal detectors, waiting to get through.

Melody stumbled against a partially burned tire, the rank smell of charred rubber and tear gas still lingering in the air. "Careful, I want to show you something," Mahmoud said.

They continued walking until they turned into a busy Palestinian market, light filtered through the wire mesh over them, metal slabs and tarps thrown above the rows of shops. Melody walked by carts piled high with cucumbers, tomatoes, peppers, dates, shelves of glassware, mounds of cheap pants, tee shirts, underwear. She inhaled the dank aromatic smell from large open sacs of spices, cardamom, cinnamon, wide burlap bags of almonds and chickpeas. An old man with a cane, wearing a checkered keffiyeh secured with a circle of black rope around his head, hobbled by and stopped in front of a shop selling brightly colored cushions.

Mahmoud paused. "Look up." Melody craned her head skyward. Cradled in the wire mesh above the shops were rocks, bricks, bottles, piles of plastic bags and trash. "See, the settlers live right above the market-place." Mahmoud shook his head. "They throw that garbage, and also urine, feces, even bleach and acid, on the Palestinian shoppers below."

Melody took out her phone. Click. Click. Click. A faint, acidy nausea gurgled into the back of her throat again. *Aaron, Aaron, Aaron.* She shook her head.

"They are suffocating us."

Melody just stood still gaping and taking photos.

"We've seen enough. Let's go. We need to get to Yasmina's."

As they stepped out of the market, a young man in jeans wearing a kippah, tzitzit dangling from his shirt, strode up to Melody. "You!" He pointed at her. "Are you with that Arab?"

"Me? What?" Melody stiffened with fear.

Mahmoud grabbed her hand. "Come, let's go."

She tossed her head. "No, this isn't right." A wave of rage and disbelief shook her out of her terror. She stared at the settler, her mind jumbled by his sneering aggression, the craziness of the market, the racist graffiti. "You're Jewish?"

The young man glared at her. "I said, are you with that dirty Arab? You gonna answer?"

Melody felt her head exploding. She couldn't control her tongue. "You believe in god?" Her outrage burst out of her like uncontrolled fireworks. "What would he think of your behavior?"

"Fuck your G-d!" The young man lunged toward Mahmoud.

"Sir, we are leaving. No trouble. No trouble." Mahmoud put his hand up. "Please." He tugged on Melody's hand, his eyes stern. "Now!" He pulled at her hand again and they both turned and walked away. "Don't run, just keep your eyes down and walk."

"You will pay! Fuck you!" the young man yelled. "Stinking dirty Arab!" He pulled out his cellphone and gestured.

At the next corner, an Israeli soldier appeared. "Papers?"

Mahmoud stopped, took out his ID, and handed them to the soldier. "Passport?"

Melody fumbled for her passport.

"Wait here."

Mahmoud turned toward Melody. "Say nothing. Understood?"

Melody nodded. Her insides quaked and her mouth went dry. She just wanted to bolt, fast, away from this street, from this city. She willed her legs to stay still.

The soldier returned with his papers. "You may go."

The pattern repeated itself every few blocks until they reached the car. Papers, passport, wait, dread, go.

When Melody saw the taxi, she ran, grabbed the door, and crawled quickly into her seat. "Oh my god, oh my god. What just happened? I'm sorry, I'm soooo sorry."

Mahmoud turned to her. "My dear, the settlers talk to the soldiers, they all work together. Praise be to Allah we are safe. You are brave but crazy. This could have ended badly." He reached for a cigarette.

Melody nodded vigorously, eyes wide. "I'm sorry. I, I just couldn't stand how he was treating you."

"You see, this place could make you angry. And reckless, yes?" Mahmoud started the ignition. "Let's get to your Yasmina's house." He turned the car around. As they headed down the street, Melody noticed a slab of concrete, spray-painted, DISMANTLE THE GHETTO: TAKE THE SETTLERS OUT OF HEBRON. Click. A donkey loaded with large bundles of straw, a man bouncing on its back, trotted by. Click.

"Wait, could you stop the car." Melody leaned out the window. A man wearing a kippah was pointing his gun at a young boy cowering against a wall. Click. "Let's go." *I gotta talk to Aaron. Wait 'til he sees this.*

Chapter Twenty-Four

KANAFE

ELODY STOOD OUTSIDE THE TAXI AND STARED. Her heart thumped wildly. She was finally going to see Yasmina, but so much had happened since her initial frantic bus ride from Jerusalem. And now, she was really here, with her best friend, in front of her uncle's house. Melody bit her lip and fumbled with her bracelet. *Maybe Yasmina's angry with me for coming? Maybe she's hiding something? Is there something she can't tell me? Maybe I shouldn't tell her about the almost rape when she's got all this other stuff going on.* Melody stepped onto the walkway lined with almond, lemon, and fig trees drooping with fruit, her red sneakers crunching on the stones. As she tugged on her baseball cap and took a few steps toward the house, the door opened slowly.

Melody looked at Yasmina. She seemed thinner. A muscle in her face twitched uncontrollably. She leaned on the heavy carved door and waved slowly at her uncle, Mahmoud. Suddenly her eyes crinkled up and she smiled. "Come here, you crazy friend."

Melody exhaled a deep sigh of relief and walked slowly toward the door, lugging her backpack. *Please oh please oh please be okay.* She hugged Yasmina cautiously as if she were afraid her friend would break. "You made it in one piece? Come upstairs. Meet my family. I'm warning you, there are a lot of them and everyone wants to see you. You're kind of a celebrity."

Oh great. This could be awkward. All I want to do is talk talk talk with Yaz. In private. Do they have privacy here? Melody took a deep breath and turned around to wave goodbye to Mahmoud.

"My uncle lives on the second floor. His son Fouad and family live downstairs and his other son, Abdallah and his family live upstairs. It's kind of a family compound."

"Okaaay." Melody waved one more time to Mahmoud. She called out, "Thank you. You were a really great tour guide. And restaurant. And you probably kept me out of trouble or prison or something."

Mahmoud winked, "No problem, no problem," puffed on his cigarette, and turned to walk toward his house down the street.

Yasmina gave Melody a funny look. "Prison? What have you two been up to?"

Melody shrugged. "Checking out Hebron."

"Oh really? Did Mahmoud give you the grand tour?" Yasmina gestured for her to come up the stone steps into the second floor apartment. They walked through an arched doorway into a spacious living room, with richly upholstered furniture, the wood dark with heavy carved legs, three couches piled with embroidered cushions, bowls of almonds on the end tables. "This is my uncle, Kareem Khdour, and my sitti, I mean my grandma, everyone calls her Um Kareem, that means mother of Kareem."

Melody felt suddenly shy. *Do I shake his hand? Hug him? Bow? Maybe these guys do that kissing thing? It all felt so formal.* Kareem sat regally on the couch, wearing a gray suit, a crisp white shirt open at the neck, thick black chest curls popping through, one pant leg partially rolled up. He propped his back against some cushions and rubbed his injured leg, the heavy cast rested on a chair. Hardware protruded through the plaster. Melody winced. "Marhaba and welcome to my home, Miss Melody. Don't worry about my leg. Just an injury. Surgery too. I will be better. I understand you are a friend of Yasmina?"

Melody smiled and nodded. She rattled her bracelet around her wrist a few times. "I hope you're feeling better. Sir. Yes, thank you. I mean, I am Yaz's friend. From Vermont. We've known each other since forever. She's like my sister."

"Sit down, please." Kareem nodded toward a chair next to Um Kareem and stroked his mustache. "My mother doesn't speak English, but she is happy to meet you." Melody smiled at the elderly woman, her tiny body draped with a delicately embroidered long dress and cream-colored hijab. The older woman ran her fingers over and over wooden prayer beads and when she smiled at Melody her face wrinkled like crumpled parchment paper.

Wow, she's like Biblically old. As Melody sat down at the edge of her chair, Yasmina's aunt came bustling in carrying a tray of tiny cups of thick black coffee and glasses of orange juice. "Hello, welcome, I am Sara, and this is my daughter Rana, she has the cookies, and Huda who is bringing the sugar and the kanafeh." She put the tray down and bent over Melody, kissing her on each cheek. "You'll meet Marium later, she's taking a computer course." As if on cue, the front door opened and two young men came in, holding a soccer ball. "And these are my sons Omar and Abdallah." They draped themselves over a smaller couch and sat arm in arm. Sara turned and called to another room. "Fouad, we have company. Come in here."

How am I going to remember all these people? Melody's head throbbed. *Okay, Kareem, Sara, Rana...* "Nice to meet you." Melody nodded tentatively at each smiling face. The door opened again and Mahmoud appeared, grinning broadly.

"Brother, you need to call this young lady's father and tell him all is well." He handed Kareem a slip of paper with the phone number. "His name is Phillip. Melody, I want you to meet my daughters, Noura, Raeda, Lama, and Esmat."

Melody nodded at the older teenagers. *Oh god, more names.*

"Their English is getting better. They want to practice on you."

The four young women smiled and one asked slowly, "I am Noura. You are from America? Your hair is very red."

Before Melody could answer, a young man with laughing eyes and thick black hair cruised into the room, pushing himself in a wheelchair. "Fouad, this is Yasmina's friend from the US." Sara turned to Melody. "Please dear, have something to eat, you must be hungry. Do you like figs? From our fig tree?"

Melody was trying to think of a way to remember everyone's name while answering all their questions. *Kangaroo-Kareem, Squirrel-Sara, Rhino-Rana. She thought about taking out her notebook and just writing them all down with little cues.*

1. *Rana cookies, laughing eyes.*
2. *Huda sugar, thick eyebrows.*
3. *Marium computers.*
4. *Omar taller than Abdallah, with mustache.*
5. *Um Kareem sounds like Kareem only smaller.*

Would that be rude? She reached for the cookies. "What's kanafeh?"

"A lovely pastry, dear, made with cheese and pistachios, soaked in sugary syrup. Very special. Here's a plate and a fork, have some. Do you drink coffee? Arabic coffee is very strong."

As Melody watched Sara spoon in the sugar, she thought, *Oh god, strong coffee with lots of sugar. I'll have a frigging seizure.*

"Perhaps you want tea? Dear, have some tea."

That sounds safer. "Sure, thank you. And I'll try the kanafeh. And a fig." *Maybe if I keep stuffing my mouth, no one will expect me to talk.* Melody stared at Yasmina with a pleading can't-you-save-me-from-all-your-relatives kind of look.

Yasmina got up and sat on the ottoman in front of Melody. "Noura, come see Melody's photos. She has a really cute dog."

Thank you thank you thank you. Melody opened her phone and scrolled through her pictures, past Hebron, Bethlehem, Tel Aviv, Jerusalem, back to her old life in Vermont. It didn't look that complicated now. "This is Cheddar, my puppy." The dog's warm brown eyes filled her with a yearning for her home, her bed, her messy room. Noura, Raeda, Lama, and Esmat clustered around and suddenly everyone was talking. Mostly in Arabic. Melody leaned forward and reached for more cookies, nodding as if she were following the conversation.

A barefoot little boy appeared at the door. Yasmina stretched out her hand. "Yallah, come here sweetie, sit on my lap." Yasmina looked at Melody. "This is Majed, Fouad's little boy. He's four." The boy scrambled up on her knee and stared shyly at Melody, eyes as big and brown as a fawn. He took a cookie from Yasmina and snuggled deeply into her lap.

Sara poured Melody another cup of tea. "You must be exhausted. I'll show you your room soon, you will be sleeping with Yasmina and Rana and Huda. Marium will sleep in Sitti's room.

"Oh no, really, I don't want to throw anyone out of their bed."

"No problem. Come dear." She smiled, eyes warm and playful. "But first," she stepped back as if she had discovered a terrible mistake. "You must have more kanafeh. You haven't eaten enough. Then you can rest until dinner. But tell me, how is your family?"

Oh wow. There's going to be more food? Melody loaded up her plate, thinking maybe she could stash it away for a midnight snack. She thought about her pitifully small, boring family. What could she say?

"Well…my father is in Jerusalem at a conference, I'm sure Yasmina told you. He's a college professor in Vermont, archeology. He's always talking about ancient Middle Eastern something or other. My mom, well you know she died, but she was a music teacher. No brothers or sisters, but I have a dog." Melody smiled expectantly. *Should I keep on talking?* Sara nodded.

"My mom's sister lives in Jaffa, Jaffa/Tel Aviv. With her kids and her husband. Says she fell in love with Israel during her junior year abroad. Hebrew University. Then she fell in love with this guy in her program. Married him." Melody stopped to take a bite of kanafeh. "Wow, that's amazingly delish." Sara smiled and everyone looked at Melody. *Okay... they want more?*

"So, my family. My aunt told me she loves hiking. She's in tech now. They have two kids. A daughter and..." Melody's jaw clenched. She glanced at Yasmina. "A son. He's in the army. I don't really know them well." Melody felt like she had said way too much already but she couldn't stop. She needed them to know something about her, to not feel invisible. "I live in a college town, small, lots of trees, kind of quiet. Yaz and I play basketball." *Stop with the verbal diarrhea already. What's wrong with you? TMI. TMI.* Melody made her friendly guest kind of face. "Have you been to Jaffa?"

Painful silence

"I'm looking forward to meeting your father." Sara busied herself with some plates.

Melody winced. Her brain registered a silent scream of disapproval. *You-are-such-a-jerk.*

Sara looked up. "Oh, dear, you must be tired. Come with me." Melody exhaled sharply, silently beating herself for the Jaffa question, and followed Sara out the door into the hall. You idiot, of course they can't get permits. Jaffa is in Israel, dimwit. She got the distinct impression that they would treat her kindly no matter what kind of a dumbass she was. Also, saying no thank you to another helping would definitely be rude. Melody half smiled. *Like first I had no family and now I'm drowning in one. But kind of in a good way. In a too-much-food-is-love kind of way. I really have to pee. All that tea. I hope they have bathrooms here. I mean, the flush kind. Or really, at this point, any kind will do.*

Melody felt a sticky little hand reaching for hers. "Hello, little guy. You been eating kanafeh? Let's go check out my room. Then maybe we can find a bathroom and wash your hands. Yallah."

Chapter Twenty-Five

OLIVE TREE

I T WAS LATE AND MELODY FELT LIKE A GIANT BLIMP, stuffed with eggplant and maqluba. *That's not just some ordinary kind of chicken and rice. It's addictive. What do they put in it? Cocaine?* She had finally figured out that if she didn't eat everything on her plate, no one would keep refilling it. A major dilemma because she really wanted to eat everything, the whole overflowing pot. She wished she had strategized earlier in the evening. Before her clothes got too tight.

She was now sitting in the living room yearning to loosen her belt buckle and fill her lungs. Even a little gasp would feel better. She was holding her notebook, reconstructing everyone's name and who was related to whom, as clusters of family chattered, texted, shared YouTube videos. The adults sipped coffee while the grandmother dozed, her breath a low snore. A TV gurgled in the background, with occasional sweeping dramatic music, something from Egypt. There were a number of small children doing a puzzle and throwing plastic blocks at each other. *Who did they belong to?* Melody was not having much luck in her family tree project; her mind kept wandering to that afternoon in Tel Aviv. She cornered Yasmina in the kitchen, washing dishes. "Yaz, I really gotta tell you something."

"What is it?" Yasmina sponged another plate.

"Not here."

Yasmina gave her a questioning look.

"Got any place we could be alone?"

"Ahh." Yasmina rinsed her hands and dried them on a dishtowel. "Hey Rana, can you finish the dishes? I've got to chat with my friend. Alone."

"Better be serious if I'm gonna take your turn at the dishes." Rana laughed. "Sure."

They headed out the back door, down stone stairs next to a ramp for the wheelchair, onto a sloping grove of olive trees. The sun was setting, making long spider leg shadows wobbling over the rocky soil. "Come, I have a favorite place for sitting." When they reached a thick old olive tree with a wide split in the trunk at waist level, Yasmina hoisted herself up and gestured to Melody. "This is my thinking spot. Come on up." She stopped and looked carefully at her friend. "So, what happened? Why are you here? What couldn't wait?"

Melody loosened her belt, heaved herself skyward and settled on the opposite branch. She took a deep breath, relishing the stillness, taking in the silvery leaves and the unripe olives hanging on every branch like a thousand green tear drops. She rubbed the tiny hollows and crevices in the tree bark, inlaid with tens of little stones. *Maybe I shouldn't dump this on Yasmina.*

"This olive tree is over a thousand years old. Imagine what she has seen." Yasmina smiled. "In Palestine, we give our trees women's names and love them like members of our family."

The night air was fragrant with something that felt intoxicating; goats bleated in the distance. Beyond the olive trees, grapevines snaked through a long arbor way arching down the hill. "Wow, wow, wow, Yaz. It's like heaven, I mean if I believed in heaven."

"Pretty sweet, Mel. A real contrast to the Old City of Hebron, Huh? You saw the marketplace and everything?"

Melody nodded. A smattering of stars caught her eyes through the twisting tree branches.

"So, what's up?"

Melody wrapped her legs around the sturdy branch. She turned her gaze to Yasmina. The softness of her voice. The warmth of her eyes. That feeling of safety. Melody's legs tightened. She felt this pressure rising from her belly, through her chest, sticking in her throat. She remembered the rough hand on her breast and the smell of beer and weed. Somewhere deep inside of her, a howl exploded, a raw choking sob. "I, I, I shouldn't tell you. You've got enough to deal with." She wrapped her hands over her face and sobbed.

"What? Of course you can tell me." Yasmina patted her leg gently. "What is it? What is it? You're scaring me."

Melody felt the heat of her hand, the relief of human touch, the quiet of the evening, like even the stars had stopped to listen. Melody's body shook uncontrollably. "I shouldn't have gone to the apartment," she gasped. "I shouldn't have smoked. He was such a fucking bastard."

Yasmina leaned forward and held her tightly. "Oh baby, you're okay now. Tell me, Mel. Tell me everything."

Chapter Twenty-Six

WHITE GIRL

THEY WALKED SLOWLY BACK TO THE HOUSE, Yasmina's arm around Melody. Melody's mascara was dribbled all over her cheeks, her eyes glistening and red. She stopped and blew her nose, the light from the kitchen dappled over her body.

"Wait, let me wipe your face. You're a mess." Yasmina tenderly dabbed her friend's skin and then kissed her on the forehead. "That's better." She gave her a gentle hug. "Let's go hang in my bedroom. It's too dark out here to see each other."

Yaz sat on her bed, next to the beds of her three cousins, all in a neat row like a plate of stuffed grape leaves. She patted the bed nearest to hers and said, "This is yours." She unclipped her hijab, pulled off her under-scarf, and tossed them on the thick My Little Mermaid bedspread. Yasmina shook her head as she let her hair loose and it cascaded down her back, thick, shiny, a luminous black waterfall.

Melody plopped down opposite, knees just touching her friend, curly red hair escaping everywhere, like a cartoon character plugged into an electric socket. "So Yaz, now it's your turn. Why didn't you tell me? Your life here. The soldiers and the settlers. The checkpoints. Your uncle's arrests, his blown-up leg. You kept this all hidden..." She looked at Yasmina's face. "Like your secretly gorgeous hair under that hijab."

Yasmina locked eyes with Melody. *Thunderbolt eyes* thought Melody. *She goes from mama bear to raging tiger in a split second. Who is she?*

"Look Mel, this is hard. I live in two very different, clashing worlds. In Vermont, I can keep this all hidden."

"Yeah, but I'm your friend. You're like a different person when it comes to life here."

"I just need to live my life, wherever I am." Yasmina glanced up at the red embroidery hanging on the wall, a traditional Palestinian wedding party. "You know the *Me* in Vermont. College town. Green grass. Friendly people."

"I know that."

"You are my *little* sister. Your mom was dying. I couldn't burden you. None of the other kids would understand anyway."

"Yaz, you had this whole secret place, you never let me in. You were always Ms. Cheery Pie and Ms. Go Getter. Marching forward. Did you ever look back?"

"Ouch. I didn't have to look back. I just had to Skype my family. Like every week. Hear my uncle sobbing on the phone, my cousins struggling to get to school, my sitti unable to get her meds. Come on. I wanted to protect you. My world hurts and it's dangerous, Mel."

"Duh."

"And part of me is like you, I grew up in the States. I got my dreams. I want to go to college, play basketball, find a good boyfriend." She smiled. "A good Muslim boyfriend. I just want to fit in." Her voice cracked. "I just couldn't be thinking about this life here all the time and living in that life, so predictable, so much safer, no soldiers."

Melody put her hand on Yasmina's knee.

"I mean, we talk with my uncle every week, but..." She picked up her scarf and folded it carefully. "For a long time, I couldn't stop worrying about him and my dead cousin. Even all my cousins...the ones who aren't detained..." she paused. "Or dead...yet. I just know bad things are going to happen to some of them. And I'm gonna be safe, 6,000 miles away. It's just not fair." She shook her head, eyes brimming with tears. Melody leaned forward and stroked her cheek.

"My sitti has suffered so much. And now she's sick, losing weight. Don't even ask me about healthcare here. I feel like I can never take a deep breath, let my guard down. Back home, I couldn't concentrate at school, just hearing about things here. So I tried to put it all in a box, shoved it under my bed."

"I get that. But then everything creeps out and bites your butt while you're trying to sleep."

"And now, being here. I feel guilty that I can just get on a plane, abandon my family. It's gonna be so hard to leave."

"Oh Yaz, I am so sorry."

"And all the IDs and permits and closures and Israeli soldiers invading the house, trashing the kitchen, the bedrooms." She shook her head. "Like spilling all the flour on the floor and pouring oil on it. Breaking the kitchen chairs. Just living here, as well as resisting all this…violence and hate…comes with a price, you know." She stared back at Melody. "My Uncle Kareem, he's a journalist, he's very outspoken."

"I heard."

"The Israelis hate him. Even the Palestinian Authority keeps on eye on him. I can't even count the number of times he's been arrested, tortured, let go, arrested. Never any charges. And then this big injury."

"Arrested? *Tortured?* Your uncle?"

"See." Yasmina looked directly at Melody. "How could you understand this world, in Hebron, when you live in nice, peaceful, pacifist Vermont?"

"But you live there too."

Melody heard an edge to Yasmina's voice. "Cows, perfect white snow, Ben and Jerry's ice cream. You're in a bubble, Mel. A very privileged bubble."

"What the fuck!" Melody pulled her legs up onto her bed. "My mother had cancer. She died. My father's practically…dead on arrival. I'm a frigging orphan, Yaz. And America is not exactly perfect." She leaned over and grabbed a pillow. Punched it. "Global warming, Black Lives Matter. Me Too movement. Homelessness. Hungry families. Crappy racist institutions."

"But Mel…"

"And then this awfulness in Tel Aviv. Please."

"You got your father in one piece." Melody winced. "You should talk to him. He's alive. No bullet wounds. No tear gas. No life-threatening injuries. You turn on the faucet. You got water. You turn on your computer. You got electricity." Yasmina's voice exploded. "You go to school and no one calls you Osama Bin Laden's mother. You walk outside, you don't get shot." Yasmina's face tensed. "You're a red-haired WHITE GIRL."

Melody squinted her eyes and looked at Yasmina. "Do I know you? You mean I haven't suffered enough to understand your suffering?"

Melody glared at Yasmina. Yasmina stared back. Silence.

"Look. This is not some kind of contest. Our suffering is not the same." Yasmina gazed up at the ceiling and followed a tiny crack in the plaster. "I'm sorry. I need you to accept that my hurt is different from yours. You can never fully understand it." Her face softened.

"But I still do love you, sister sister. I want to be here for you, always. Really." Yasmina grabbed Melody's hand. "I don't know how to keep my two worlds in one body, my body. I feel like Humpty Dumpty about to fall and crack in a zillion pieces. Or maybe more like any minute I'm about to step on an IED and get blown apart."

"I-E-D?"

Yasmina said this very slowly like she was taking to a child. "Improvised. Explosive. Device." She raised her eyebrows and tilted her head. "War zone?"

"That's pretty gory. And fatal." Melody's jaw relaxed. She stroked her nose ring.

"Exactly."

"So Vermont is like…a refuge?"

"Kinda. I'm at peace there, if I ignore the racism. Trying to do well at school, trying to be a good Muslim. But really, I'm just struggling to keep it all together, wherever I am, Mel. I'm doing the best I can."

Melody flinched when her phone dinged. She looked at the message. "Oh shit, it's Aaron. He's freaking out. Look, he's threatening to call his cousin if he doesn't hear from me now."

"What?"

"Yaz, that Kiryat Arba cousin, do you think he could get soldiers or even his settler thugs to come here, hurt your family? What could they do? Kidnap me? Shoot you?"

Yasmina rolled her eyes. "You better answer lover boy before he does something really dangerous. For both of us."

Chapter Twenty-Seven

GAS THE ARABS

MELODY PACKED SOME PILLOWS AGAINST the wall and quickly wiggled into a comfortable position. She heard chatter from the kitchen and the clanking of pots, a whiff of apple flavored tobacco drifted into her room. She spotted a giant, smiling Mickey Mouse waving on the bedspread under her butt, grimaced, and ran her fingers through her hair. *This is gonna be painful. Better call off the settler dogs first.* She cradled her phone and hunched over the screen, thumbs flying.

Aaron, STOP! DON'T CALL ANYONE. OK? Melody closed her eyes. A film of sweat dampened her armpits. *Please get this message and calm down. Pleaaase.*

Mel, thank G-d ur alive. Sooo worried 🙇 *Couldn't wait till morning. UP ALL NIGHT!!! I REALLY CARE ABOUT U.*

He's gonna bite off all his fingernails. Maybe his toenails too. So acting like a jerk.

Relax. I'm alive. They've been feeding me - so stuffed I can barely move. I love maqluba. Burp.

Not funny. Thought something bad happened to u. Ur staying with Yaz, right, with that Arab family??? That's dangerous. Ur Jewish remember? They hate Jews - do they know who you are?

Arghhh. Melody felt like screaming, like shaking Aaron by the shoulders and yelling, "What the fuck is wrong with you? Yaz's family welcomed me into their home, all 10,000 of them, give or take. I'm sitting on a bed with Mickey Mouse...and his mermaid girlfriend Ariel, next bed over." *For a smart kid, he sounded so brainwashed. Scared.* She scratched her head. *Prejudiced, that's the word. Prejudiced. He hates Arabs. All of them. He's frightened.* She took a long deep breath.

Aaron, you're a good person right?

Try to be. Really want to be a righteous person, like in the Torah. A tzadik, Book of Job.

Don't go all religious on me. I'm an atheist, remember?

Okay. Just saying...

Melody stared up at the ceiling. She noticed the long crack in the plaster. *Go slow and be patient. He just doesn't know.*

You believe Black people should be treated equal, right?

Course, what are u talking about?

Yaz is your friend too, right?

Yup. So?

She is an Arab?

Arab American. There are some nice ones OBVIOUSLY.

Ughhhh, he makes me so angry.

You believe people should be kind, right?

Is this a riddle or something?

You love your cousin?

You think he's living a righteous life?

Melody shook her head. "Yaz, I'm not sure how to do this. Aaron's in his own little world. He's totally, I don't know, walled in with all the gates locked."

"Just tell him what you saw. Show him your pictures. He wants to be a good person."

Yaz says hi. Her uncle's leg was just blown to bits by an armed Israeli.

What was he doing? They don't just shoot people for nothin u know.

Melody stopped. *Isn't that what Black Lives Matter is all about? Just shooting people? For nothing? Aaron sounds so....so racist.* She rubbed her nose ring and bent over the phone. *He's a journalist. He was reporting.*

I'm sure he was doing something.

Melody crossed her eyes and glared at Yasmina. "He doesn't get it." Yasmina gestured, taking a pretend photo on her phone.

Sharing some photos of my trip. Not exactly a sunny Mediterranean vacation. Melody started scrolling through her pictures.

Wall around Bethlehem, aka fence. Concrete. 24 feet high. Huge military terminal to get in or out. Fucking prison. Not like Christmas cards and baby Jesus.

Mel, what is wrong with u? Built wall to keep suicide bombers out & it worked. They want to destroy Israel. Toss Jews into the sea. IF THEY DON'T KILL US FIRST!!!

Melody wiggled toward the edge of the bed, revealing the full Mickey Mouse. She stroked his nose slowly. *What would you do, my little Mickey Mouse?* She turned on her side, the phone in her hand, and started tapping.

Palestinian village. Water tanks on roof. Israel controls water. Constant shortages. Arroub Refugee Camp, people very poor, refugees from 1948 war, Jewish settlements encircle the hills. She stared at the face of a young child standing next to the barbed wire fencing, smiling, barefoot.

All that land was promised to THE JEWISH PEOPLE BY G-D, plus we WON the war. TWICE! Arabs have 22 countries they can go to. THIS IS ALL WE'VE GOT. Come on, are u brainwashed or something?

Melody looked at the empty market in Hebron, shop doors welded closed, awful graffiti. *Market in Old Hebron, Palestinians run out by Israeli settlers.*

She waited for a response. What's he thinking? Ten seconds. Twenty seconds.

Is that a Star of David spray-painted on door?

Yup. Symbol of THE JEWISH PEOPLE. What do you think?

Aaron went totally silent. She could almost hear him deliberating, wincing, rubbing the back of his neck, uncomfortably squirming. *There was something about that imagery, like swastikas on Jewish shops in Germany. Awful, awful, terrifyingly awful.*

She sent him the picture of the door sprayed, GAS THE ARABS. *Think your cousin did that?*

Come on Mel, he's not like that. Trust me.

Melody felt her face flush. *Come on Aaron, just admit this is not okay.* She scrolled through more photos.

Palestinian homes encased in wire mesh-protect from rock throwing settlers.

*Palestinian market, check out wire mesh. Settlers live above the market, throw bricks, rocks, garbage, *shit* *acid* on shoppers below.*

Stop Mel, where's your info from??? This is clash of civilizations. Arabs are not the good guys. They massacred Jews in Hebron FYI, there's gotta be good reasons for what ur seeing. Did you visit any settlers?

Melody stared at Yaz. "He wants to know if I talked with any settlers." Yasmina rolled her eyes.

My cousin says they're really nice and proud to be Jews, doing G-d's work.

Melody felt a shiver of rage. *One settler, yelled and cursed me for being friendly with a Palestinian taxi driver.*

Did you do something? Are u nuts? Bottom line. When push comes to shove, I stand with Jews. They're my people *and urs if u would let them be.*

Melody punched the pillow at the end of the bed again. She grabbed her phone. *Throwing acid on shoppers? Screaming at me? Nice people? They're racists!!!!*

Melody stared at the next photo. It was the last one she had taken. The man wearing a kippah, gun pointed at the young boy cowering against a wall. The boy was crying. A woman's mouth was grimacing in a scream and she was pulling on the boy's shirt. *Is Aaron ready for this? Will I freak him out? Lose him as a friend? Am I pushing too far? Too fast?*

Her head throbbed. The fear in the boy's eyes grabbed her. *What if I had a little brother? Oh my god, I should have said something. But what could I say? What would have happened to Mahmoud? Will Aaron stop talking to me? He's gotta see this.*

She hit send. *Street scene.* Along with the photo, Dismantle the Ghetto, slab of concrete.

Total silence. Melody exhaled loudly. She traced her finger around Mickey Mouse's ears. Then his nose again. She nibbled on a cuticle and played with her bracelet.

Yaz gave her a questioning look, eyebrows raised. "MIA?" Yaz reached over and patted her shoulder. "Do you think something you said touched a nerve?" Melody tapped on her phone, her face flushed.

What's so Jewish about tormenting a little boy? These settlers are more like skinheads or the Ku Klux Klan than your idea of a righteous person.

An ominous quiet enveloped the room. Melody pulled on her curls for a few minutes and then crawled off the bed and started pacing, stopping at each bed, checking her phone, staring at the bedspreads, Donald Duck, Anna, then back to Ariel and Mickey. She could hear her pulse pounding in her head. Finally her phone pinged.

Mel, stop.That Israeli man is my cousin.

Melody froze, her hand shook. *His cousin? Damn.*

"Yaz, look at this!"

Yaz peered at her screen. "Oh my God." She slapped her hand across her mouth. "The Kiryat Arba cousin?"

Melody shook her head slowly, deliberately. "Bingo." Her thumbs started tapping, faster and faster, the fury rising in her chest. *Your cousin may think he is doing the right thing for his people, but he is attacking a little boy, that's probably his mom, pleading for his life. Is that ok with you?*

Aaron waited to reply. *Always a reason, maybe the boy threw a rock at him. They do that. A lot.*

Melody didn't wait. *He's a grown man with a gun assaulting a little boy. Is that like in the Ten Commandments?*

STOP. Can't do this. I'm done. Conversation over.

Chapter Twenty-Eight

TRIBAL

MELODY GLARED AT HER PHONE. She bit her fingernail and leaned against the wall. "Yaz, now I've really upset him. I don't know what to do."

"You freaked him out. But in a good way. I'm sure he'll think about everything. At his own pace."

Melody's voice exploded. "The problem is that I'm not done." She looked up at the rich reds and blacks of the embroidery hanging on the wall, the photo of Al Aqsa Mosque, the poster of some Arab pop star with thick wavy hair and a million-dollar smile. "I don't want to lose him as a friend, but I can't exactly un-see what I saw. And the look on that little boy..." She handed her phone to Yasmina who gazed at the photo and nodded slowly. Melody noticed a thin rim of tears smudging her friend's eyes. "Give me back my phone. I got more to say."

Melody took a slow, intense breath. Her fingers flew.

How can you defend something if it means making lives miserable for the people who already live here?

She paced the length of the room, stopped at the window hung with thick drapes, and looked out at the dark shadows and eerily twisted branches of olive trees, grabbing at the moon.

Wouldn't you fight back if someone stole your house? Melody sat down on the bed and waited. Yasmina took a brush out of a small bedside cabinet and began brushing Melody's hair. Melody caught the floral fragrance of Yasmina's shampoo.

"Yaz, you're always in motion. Do you ever stop?" Melody tapped the bedspread with her fingers.

"I can't just sit still. Besides, these curls are out of control." Yasmina smiled. "Doing something, *anything*, helps my nerves." Her forehead crunched with concentration.

"You're changing the subject. But if you are interested, my nutso curls are why I wear a hat. With your hijab, you never have a bad hair day. Just a bad hijab day."

Yasmina laughed and began seriously brushing out the knots. "When was the last time you tamed this tangle?"

"Ouch, gently."

They both jumped when the phone pinged.

Israel plays by the rules.

Melody touched her bracelet and locked eyes with Yasmina. "He's back."

What rules???? You can't close your eyes just because you don't want to believe what your eyes are telling you. I'm sure there are lots of Israelis who think these folks are nuts, but this?

Judea and Samaria homeland to the Jewish people.

Melody leaped off the bed and the brush fell on the floor with a clunk. "I can't stand this." She picked up her phone.

No, Aaron. Forget the polemics. People are getting hurt here. You're on the wrong side.

Suddenly the phone rang, piercing the air. Aaron's voice sounded agitated. Maybe crying agitated.

"My mom would kill me if she knew I was actually calling you. Mel, I'm so…upset. I can't believe this." He paused. "The Jews are my people. We need a state that is ours. We need a safe place."

"But Aaron…"

"It's a real dangerous world, and Israel is in a dangerous neighborhood – it's not Vermont you know. And you can never forget what the Germans did."

Melody pulled at her hair. "Aaron, you have beautiful dreams and good values, and you know there is a right and wrong. The Palestinians are not the Germans. Come on. Wake up. The Nazis did terrible things to Jews. But now, 21st century, there is a right side and a wrong side here. Think about it."

Melody sat down on the Donald Duck bed and rocked back and forth. She tapped mute and looked at Yasmina. "How does a guy obsessed with god think this way?"

"Mel, think about what happens if he challenges his temple, his family, the beliefs he was brought up with."

Melody gave her a quizzical look.

"We are all tribal. You want him to defy his tribe? He's got a lot to lose, even if he's so wrong."

"Yaz, I think losing his, what do they call it? His moral compass, is even worse. Especially if the guy wants to be a rabbi."

She unmuted her phone and inhaled deeply. "Aaron, I know this is hard, but I really want you to struggle with everything I am saying and what the pictures are saying." She stopped and looked at Yasmina. "Because you are a decent person and I really like you. But what exactly is Jewish about settlers in Hebron, or checkpoints, or young men with ginormous guns who hate Arabs? Is that what your god wants? Is that how the Torah says to live?"

Aaron paused. "I really don't know what to say Mel. I'm kind of shaking inside. You scare me...This scares me."

"Good." Melody stood up and started pacing again. "Look, we all want to be good people, make good decisions, but sometimes the good decisions are the hardest of all. You have to risk something, Aaron." She stopped pacing and leaned against Yasmina. "Maybe challenge where you're coming from."

"I can't believe your saying that." Aaron's voice cracked.

Is he crying? "What does it mean to be religious if you are not kind to people who are oppressed? If you're the oppressor?"

"But the Nazis, anti-Semitism..." Melody could hear him clearly crying.

"We Jews need to stand up for ourselves."

"Is that what is happening in Hebron, Aaron? Really? If you do not make the world a kinder place for everyone, then what is the struggle for righteousness about? Isn't that what we want, you, me, Yaz? Together."

"I, I just don't know. The pictures are so upsetting. How do I know what to believe? How *can* I believe? Would G-d let Jews, his chosen people, behave this way? I don't know Mel. I just don't know."

"Good, Aaron. If you care about me, think about it."

She plopped down on the Little Mermaid bed.

"And don't listen to your cousin, okay?"

Yasmina put her arm around Melody. "Good work sister."

Chapter Twenty-Nine

TOMATO TEAM

MELODY TOSSED HER RED CURLS BACK AND CLAPPED, deeply happy despite the splash of mosquito bites blurring her freckles and the soreness in her hands and forearms. She couldn't quite believe Yaz's entire family had just canned fifty glass juice bottles of tomatoes. Ripe tomatoes. Fat, juicy but not too squishy, fire engine red. She had teased the older male cousins as they unloaded the crates, each one jousting to carry the heaviest box. She insisted she was just as strong, lifting a crate out of the packed car and tossing the tomatoes into buckets of water.

The guys had clapped, laughed, and chanted, "Girl power. Girl power." Melody had jumped up and down, her fist high in the air, pleased to be strong and useful. She marveled at the whole intense choreographed backyard production, everyone with a job, everyone enveloped in the sweet, slightly acid fragrance of fresh sunbaked tomatoes.

Melody turned to Mahmoud. "Where'd you get these?"

"Jenin. It's a city, maybe one hundred miles north, Northern West Bank."

"You would know." Melody smiled. "I bet you have driven every inch of the West Bank."

Mahmoud dipped his head in agreement, took out a cigarette and walked towards the flames.

Abdallah and Omar were in charge of three fire pits, piling up the wood and keeping the hot coals going, heating up the large pots mounted above. Little Majed ran as close to the fire is he dared, throwing twigs into the blaze before his mother scooped him up, distracting him with handfuls of salted pistachios. Rana tossed the washed tomatoes into a large pot of boiling water and Huda scooped them out and into a row of blenders. Marium and Noura kept the blenders churning, pouring the pulp into strainers, the blenders roaring on and off. Lama and Mahmoud gathered the strained juice and poured it into the second pot where the juice boiled for an hour or two while everyone helped scrape out the residual pulp and skin from the strainers, gathered twigs and logs for the fires, and jabbered away in Arabic.

All sweaty and industrious, Melody's job was to dip empty jars into another large pot of boiling water sitting next to the bubbling juice. She clocked three minutes on her phone, then grabbed each jar with tongs, emptied the excess water back into the pot, and placed the hot jars on a table to cool for a bit.

Sara and Esmat ladled the hot juice into the jars and closed them tightly. Abdallah picked up the heated jars, his hand wrapped in a rag, and lined them like sentries to cool on shelves under the stairs in the pantry. Melody felt like she was part of the team, the tomato team, a family production. The deep satisfaction of preparing food that would feed everyone through the winter, and of working together, wrapped her in a sense of belonging and accomplishment. She felt grounded, her war of emotions quieter, more manageable. Her rage floating skyward, swirling with the smoke. Scattering to the heavens.

Now, with the heat of the day slowly dissipating, everyone gathered in the living room, pushed their chairs against the walls, and tried to chat as Fouad pounded on the metal drumhead of his tablah, cradled between his skinny thighs. He had parked his wheelchair next to Kareen who was rapping his fingers against the armchair. The drumming was infectious. Melody tapped her feet as Fouad's fingers flew, high notes, low notes, slightly tinny bonking, trills of beats, his hands sometimes slow, fingers flat and deliberate, sometimes a blurred frenzy of movement. She could see drops of sweat gathering on his muscled forearms, glistening off the thick, black hairs, the air permeated with the sour smell of a man dripping with perspiration. His head bobbed rhythmically as his shoulders swayed. He threw his head back and started singing an undulating melody over the lively din.

Sara shooed the teenage boys and young men out of the room. "This is not for you to see. Yalla, yalla." They lined up outside in the backyard; cigarette smoke drifted into the open living room windows. Sara got up and grabbed Yasmina's hand and they started dancing, shifting from right to left foot, hips swaying slightly, hitting every other beat, waving their arms with a gentle curve of the wrist. Fouad's syncopated rhythms beckoned as Mahmoud's daughter, Noura, urged her sisters to join. Raeda and Lama giggled and stood up. Raeda held out a delicately patterned scarf, Lama took the other end, and they began to move, circling each other, eyes locked together.

Abdallah's three little kids charged into the room from upstairs and started jumping and galloping around, in sync with the pounding beats. Sitti grinned, clapped her hands, loudly ululating. Others joined in, adding to the joy of the music and the ebullience of the song.

Melody sat at the edge of her chair, clapping, bathed in the energy and good feeling. *This is what real family feels like.* A lightness in her chest lifted her mood even further. Suddenly, she felt an insistent hand on her arm. Fouad's little boy, Majed, pulled on her and wiggled his four-year-old body rhythmically. "Oh no, I really can't dance." Melody shook her head. *Really, I'm a total klutz. I'll just embarrass myself.* The boy glued his eyes to Melody's face. *Oh god, he's not going to take no for an answer.* Reluctantly she unfolded herself from the chair as he pulled her into the middle of the floor. Everyone started cheering and clapping as the drumming grew wilder and more insistent.

Rana tossed Melody another scarf as Huda and Marium swayed back and forth to the beat, grinning and whistling. Melody caught the scarf and wound it around Majed's waist as they wiggled and shimmied to the music. He laughed playfully, kicking his feet side to side, and yelled, "Thank you lady. Very good."

Rana bounced up to Melody and whispered, "Sitti says we will all dance at your wedding."

Melody laughed. "In your dreams, sweetheart!" She bent over and swung Majed up on her shoulders. He chortled with delight, grabbing a chunk of her red curls to steady himself. She held onto one of his sturdy legs and pulled out her phone, carefully balancing the boy, and took a selfie of them together. Her freckled grin, chin distorted by the closeness of the screen, Majed's round face, a tussle of black curls on top and a buzz cut on the sides. She felt content, embraced, connected, a deep peacefulness in her heart. She switched to video, tapped the red record button, and visually swept across the room. Fouad in a drumming frenzy, the women waving scarves, a little boy jumping up and down squealing. *For Aaron.*

As exhaustion set in, the music quieted. Sara retreated to the kitchen and soon brought out a tray with bowls of roasted, salted nuts: mixed pistachios, almonds, and cashews. "This is called makhluta. Try some, Melody." Sara disappeared again and returned with bottles of orange soda and Coke and a tower of paper cups.

No chance of ever getting hungry around here. Melody lifted Majed off her shoulders and collapsed with him into a deep cushioned chair. A soft landing. He cozied into her lap and started playing with her silver bracelet. Sara handed Melody a plate of salted pumpkin, sunflower, and watermelon seeds and a bowl of figs. Piles of chewed nut skins and husks collected on the side tables as everyone attacked the food. Melody listened to the gentle, satisfying music of crunching, crackling, and soft chatter.

She took a picture of the array of nuts, uploaded the photo and texted Aaron. *The food is fab. They really know how to feed me.* Send. Then she uploaded the selfie and the video. *My Hebron family.* 🌸 Melody tickled Majed, who squirmed in a mix of pleasure and pain as her fingers danced across his belly and into his armpits. As he giggled and protested, she heard a ping.

They dance????

Melody sighed deeply and shook her head, part weary, part annoyed. She put Majed down. *Of course they do. How do I explain this? Life goes on here. There's a ton of joy and love.*

She searched for an emoji of a woman in a hijab, laughing. No results. *Even the phone doesn't get it.*

Chapter Thirty

ZUCCHINI, EGGPLANT, FAVA BEANS, AND DAD

"NO MEL, HOLD YOUR HAND LIKE THIS," Yasmina said.

Melody grabbed the little zucchini in her left hand and dug the serrated vegetable corer into the end of the squash. A tiny shred of zucchini landed in the bowl. *Maybe I should use my fingernails? Or my teeth? This is impossible.* She pulled open a cabinet drawer and pulled out a paring knife.

"No, that won't work. Go deeper, like this." Yasmina twisted her wrist, making a sharp turn into her zucchini, creating a perfect tunnel of squash seeds and flesh. She repeated the twist a few times, and in seconds the zucchini was evenly cored and ready for the lamb stuffing. A zesty aroma of herbs and parsley drifted over the table as Huda chopped the freshly picked greens and lyrical oud music warbled from the kitchen radio.

Melody tried again. The tip of the corer blasted through the side of the squash. "Yaz, can't I do something else? You know I'm a great veggie chopper." Rana raised her eyebrows and giggled as she dug into a growing pyramid of purple baby eggplants.

Melody made a goofy face. "This is so frustrating. Okay Top Chef. What do I do now?"

"Try again, Anthony Bourdain," Yasmina replied, handing her another untouched little squash. "I mean Antonia."

"Yeah right." Melody grinned and took the squash. "Ahh, another victim. Sorry buddy." Huda hovered over Melody and placed her hands on Melody's, twisting and turning, twisting and turning. "Dadaaa!" Melody grinned. "See, I'm not so hopeless when I have a hands-on teacher. We could definitely do a cooking show."

Yasmina laughed. "Right, I'm sure the cooking channel would just love to film in Hebron. Their knives would never make it through a checkpoint." Her grandmother smiled and said something in Arabic.

"Sitti says she taught us everything we know. And, Mel, you will learn too. You have to persevere." Yasmina laughed. "She says it's a life lesson, steady persistence."

Her grandmother leaned into the table, rapidly shelling fava beans. Yasmina gave her a hug. Her grandmother patted her arm, face crinkling, eyes warm with pleasure, her broad smile exposing a few missing teeth. She gestured and whispered at Yasmina. "She says if you learn to do this right, you will get a good husband."

"Woah. Not so fast, Yaz." Melody put down her corer and raised her eyebrows. "Has she found you a good husband yet?"

Yasmina and her cousins chuckled. Huda waved her finger. "Yasmina says she doesn't want a husband. Not like me. I'm so happy I'm engaged." Yaz winked at Melody. "I bet Yasmina is waiting for a cute American boy."

"Tell her I'm only sixteen," said Melody.

The grandmother shook her head when Yasmina translated.

"She says, sixteen is the perfect age. You are young and beautiful. She was married at fifteen. Pregnant by sixteen. See what I mean?"

"Yeah, and that was a hundred years ago. Tell her thanks, but no thanks." Melody stared at the elderly woman's thickened, arthritic hands. "She could win a bean shelling contest with those creaky old fingers." She pointed at the basket filled with little, pale green favas, the long thin emptied shells piling up on the table and gave her a thumbs up.

"She's been making foul for over a half a century, she could do it in her sleep," Rana said, reaching for a handful of lemons.

"Foul? What's foul?" asked Melody.

"That's breakfast tomorrow, mashed up fava beans with lemon juice and crushed garlic. And of course olive oil. Yummy."

"You guys put olive oil on everything."

"It's our secret sauce." Yasmina winked.

Sara peeked through the kitchen door. "How are the cooks doing? Yasmina, ready for the lamb? Did you get the rice out? Melody, did you ever get the hang of the vegetables?"

Loud honking cut through the air and Melody stiffened. *Oh god, has it been three days already? I've been so busy with these guys I lost track of time. I bet it's my father.* Sara called out, "I'll get the door," and turned away from the kitchen.

Melody looked longingly at Yasmina. "I really don't want to go. I'm happy here. I feel like I belong. Can you hide me somewhere? Don't you have an old olive press or something out in the field, somewhere he won't find me?"

"Oh, Mel. He's your dad. I'll support you. No matter what he says."

Melody's face tightened, and she held on to her bracelet. "He's not gonna be happy." She looked down at her tattoo. "And I'm not gonna be happy either."

Melody and Yasmina washed their hands at the kitchen sink. Melody dawdled with the drying towel. "Come on Mel. Let's go. He's not going to bite you."

"You never know. He's got sharp teeth." She scowled and bared her fangs like a hungry lion.

"Oh come on, Mel. You're safe with us. We're family. Right?"

Melody exhaled slowly. "Right."

They walked toward the living room, Melody dawdling behind Yasmina. Phillip was standing uncomfortably in front of Sara, handing her a box of chocolates. Kareem was in his usual spot, leg elevated, stroking his mustache.

"I'm so very sorry my daughter barged into your home like this. I really hope she hasn't been any trouble." Phillip glanced at the richly upholstered couches, the heavy curtains, the piles of embroidered cushions.

"Oh, don't worry, she is welcome here," said Kareem.

Sara unwrapped the box and opened the top. "How thoughtful of you." She removed the paper covering; all the chocolates had melted together into a large brown blob. "No worries. It's hot this time of year."

"I'm so sorry. I didn't think…Please. Thank you so very, very much for taking care of my daughter. In your lovely home." He gestured with one hand. "In your condition." He nodded at Kareem's cast. "I hope she hasn't been an imposition. And of course, please let me pay for the taxi."

Sara smiled. "No, no. No problem, do sit down. I will get coffee."

"No, no really. We have to get going." He retreated to the arched doorway.

"Yes." Sara pointed to the couch. "Sit down. Your daughter is in the kitchen stuffing zucchinis. You have to stay for dinner."

"No really." He did a double take. "Making dinner? My daughter?"

"We're teaching her how to stuff zucchinis and eggplant." Sara laughed. "She's been so friendly and helpful. You are so lucky."

"My daughter?" Phillip sat down abruptly on the couch opposite Kareem and fidgeted with his hands. A ceiling fan stirred the warm air across his face. His neck stiffened when he heard two cats screeching loudly outside.

"Yes, Dad, your daughter," Melody said, standing in the doorway, leaning against Yasmina.

Phillip nodded at Kareem, "Excuse me." He got up, strode over to Melody, and said in a hushed, tight whisper. "Young lady, we have to talk."

Melody stared at the floor, the gold and blue patterns dancing on the Persian rug, the tip of her toe peeking through one of her red sneakers. "Here? Now?" She looked up at him, her face as blank as she could manage.

Sara bustled in with the tray of coffee, the scent of cardamom wafting past Melody and her father.

"Please sit down, Mr. Phillip. You are our guest. We want to welcome you to Hebron. I understand you are an archeologist?"

Phillip nodded uncomfortably, "Well, yes." He stared at Melody and peered over his glasses. "Later." He returned to the couch, sitting tensely on the edge. "Thank you for the coffee. You are very kind." He placed the cup on a small, ornately carved table inlaid with floral shaped ivory and ran his hand across the surface. His body relaxed. "Does this table date back to the Ottomans by any chance?"

Kareem nodded. "Passed through my family. Beautiful, isn't it?"

I love this. They're gonna keep feeding him and he's stuck here, distracted by the furniture, smiling and being all civil, when all he wants to do is yell at me. Melody smirked ever so slightly. *Just look at him. He keeps clenching his jaw. Trying so hard to smile. His red hair looks like he's on fire.*

Melody perched next to Kareem. "I'll get some cookies," said Yasmina as she turned toward the kitchen. Melody sighed and picked up an embroidered pillow. She put it on her lap and rested her elbows, balancing her chin in her cupped hands. *What a scene. Funny if it weren't so crazy. Mr. Khdour, outspoken Hebron journalist, interviews Professor Sullivan, prominent archeologist, on latest findings in Old Jerusalem. Professor Sullivan gives brief lecture and tries to get out of here with recalcitrant and unruly daughter. Haha. Ugh.*

Just when Melody felt she couldn't sit quietly for one more minute, Huda walked in holding her grandmother's arm. The elderly woman shuffled to the couch and sat next to Phillip, smiling. She leaned toward him and seized his hand, gesturing that he sit closer to her. She handed him a bowl of almonds, grabbed a handful of nuts and poured them into his other hand. She moved her own hand from the almonds to her mouth, nodding her head, encouraging him to eat. Her eyes sparkled.

Phillip smiled awkwardly, unclear if he should kiss her or shake her hand. He moved toward her and pecked her cheek. She grinned her toothless smile and said something in Arabic. Kareem laughed. "My mother says you are welcome in our home. You have a lovely daughter. She could find her a good husband."

"Ahem, that really won't be necessary." The grandmother patted his knee.

Yasmina arrived with the cookies. "Auntie, did you invite Mr. Phillip for dinner?"

"Oh, we really couldn't..." Phillip shifted uneasily. He sipped his coffee and stared at the Persian rug.

"Dad, they're inviting us to dinner. Come on. It's how people do things here. You know that. Arab generosity." Melody glared at her father.

"I don't want be any trouble, but I surely do not want us to travel back to Jerusalem late, with the checkpoints and..."

"Then you must stay overnight." Kareem smiled firmly at Phillip. "It's settled. Don't argue. Mahmoud will get you back to the Bethlehem terminal tomorrow, first thing, as soon as the checkpoint opens. You have come so far, we will show you some Palestinian hospitality. Good food, good conversation, my lovely family. No problem. We have plenty of room."

He shifted against the pillows and looked decisively at Phillip. "So, as you were saying about the conference...."

Chapter Thirty-One

SECOND CHANCES

MELODY CHEWED AS SLOWLY AS POSSIBLE, savoring the rich lemony flavors. She recognized the fruity, sour sumac and the zaatar's thyme and sesame. She surveyed the clutter of plates covering the table, scattered with remnants of eggplant, zucchini, lamb, bowls of olives, hummus, baba ghanoush, pickled radishes, thin cigar-shaped stuffed grape leaves. The family mostly ate with their fingers, scooping and sharing. Piles of olive pits collected on the edge of plates. The small mountain of fresh flat bread gradually dwindled. Bottled water with a JERICHO label and Coke wrapped in its red logo stood in the center of the table like sentries.

I hope this meal never stops. Maybe we could just coast into breakfast and I'll make my escape after that. She imagined her father round and stuffed like an eggplant, dozing off as she was smuggled away under a pile of fava beans. She played with the words full, foul, and fool. She took a long drawn-out sip of sweet tea. The last time she remembered being this quiet was that disastrous dinner in Tel Aviv with her Israeli cousins. Malkah. Melody flinched.

She licked the sticky rose water syrup off her fingers as she dawdled over her second piece of basbousa, watching her father sip a tiny cup of bitter coffee sweetened with many teaspoons of sugar. *Sugar and caffeine, he's gonna be wired. My brain is buzzing, all this chatter in Arabic and English, all the smiling and nodding. My dad's pretend happy face. I'm exhausted.* Melody felt Yasmina's foot snuggling up against her sneaker under the table. Yasmina sent her a concerned, worried look. Melody thought about how angry her father must be underneath all the pleasantries. *What's he gonna do?* She glanced at Yasmina. *Life raft. Don't leave me alone.*

Phillip cleared his throat. "Sara, that was a wonderful meal, thank you so much. And young ladies," he nodded at Rana, Huda, and Marium. "Thank you." He nodded at Melody. "You too, Mel. I am sorry Melody and I have intruded…"

"Oh please, we feel like your daughter is a member of the family. You are totally welcome here."

"Would you join me in the living room while the ladies clean up?" Kareem picked a shred of food from his teeth and unlocked his wheelchair. "Smoke some nargileh, hookah, with my sons, Abdallah and Fouad? Very relaxing at the end of a long day. They would love to practice their English, and we all want to hear more about America."

"I agree it's been a very long day." Phillip wiped his lips. "But I think I need some time with my daughter, if you will excuse us." Melody stiffened. Phillip backed his chair away from the table with an ominous rumble. Melody's heart plunged like a stone into a very deep well. She waited for the stone to hit water. "Melody?"

Melody got up reluctantly. *I'm a doomed prisoner heading straight to the guillotine.*

"Is there some place we could talk? Privately?" He stopped and looked at her. She stared blankly back, jaw tight, silent. "Let's go outside. The garden looked lovely."

Yasmina stood up quickly. "There is a quiet place out back, in the olive grove. I'll take you there." She winked at Melody.

Melody followed her father and Yasmina down the back steps, past the potted herbs. She bit her lip and held on to her bracelet. *Gang plank. I'm just gonna splash and die.* She grabbed Yasmina's hand. At the edge of the olive grove, she saw a table and several white plastic chairs. *Interrogation center.* The air was laden with that floral fragrance she could not place. Yasmina kissed her and whispered, "I'll see you soon. You've got to be honest with your dad. Be strong and be kind." Chimes tinkled from somewhere in the backyard and caged pigeons cooed in the dusky light.

Melody felt tears rimming her eyes. She sat down and stared at her father, blinking, wiping her nose on her hand. His body was outlined by rays of setting sun, his face in shadow. Darth Vader. With a girlfriend.

"Melody, you know what you did was very irresponsible. I was terrified." He exhaled sharply. "I didn't know where you were, who you were with, if you were safe." He shook his head. "You don't speak Arabic. This was very flighty, thoughtless behavior." He sat down opposite her and placed his elbow on the table. "I just don't know what to say. I'm very disappointed."

Melody sat silently, her rage and sorrow churning like lava, about to blow. The silver leaves of the olive trees around her shimmered with a slight breeze. In the distance she heard young men's voices, loud honking, laughter. An engine roared. She stared at a cluster of pebbles embedded in the twisted bark of a very old olive tree. At its based was a pile of... metal balls? She looked closer. Empty tear gas canisters.

"Mel, look at me. You have been very immature. And disrespectful. I expected so much more of you. We need to have an understanding about your behavior. I think there should be some consequences to running away..."

"My behavior?" Melody stood up abruptly. "My behavior?" She waved her arms in front of her. "Dad, when was the last time we actually talked, I mean really talked? Do you have any idea who I am?" She ran her hand brusquely through her red curls, knocking off her hat. "Do you know what is happening to me? What I'm feeling?"

"Melody!"

"Don't Melody me. You aren't here for me. It's like I'm a cardboard cutout daughter, and you lug me around when you can't leave me alone."

Phillip snorted and sat back in his chair. "That is not fair. I love you very much. I thought this trip would be an adventure. For us. To share. You had a good time with Malkah."

"Dad. What the fuck. Good time?" Melody inhaled sharply. "You have no idea what happened to me."

"What do you mean, what happened?"

Melody shook her head and went silent, her brain bursting like the tear gas canisters at the base of the tree.

Phillip's voice lowered, "Melody, answer me."

"I can't talk about it."

"It?" Phillip began to stand up, his eyebrows heading toward his receding hairline.

Melody looked through the olive trees, focusing anywhere but her father's face. The silence spread like a dense fog, enveloping both of them. Her father waited, suspended, bent over the table. It felt like forever.

"Malkah's brother."

"Daniel?"

She took a very deep breath. "Well one of his soldier buddies, he...."
She exhaled briskly. *What the fuck.* "He assaulted me at their apartment."

Her father straightened and gasped.

"That's not what I call a good time."

Phillip leaned across the table, his voice tremulous. "What! Honey.
Were you hurt? What did he do? Why didn't you tell me?"

"Because I can't, Dad. Because you are the last person in the whole
world I would tell."

"Now, Melody..."

"You're M-I-A, Dad. You've been totally absent in my life. I'm almost
raped and you didn't even notice I was dying at that stupid dinner. Dying
inside." Melody paced back and forth. "Why did you think I needed to
be with Yasmina? I was desperate. I needed a friend, a real honest friend.
I needed someone to just....just hold me." Melody choked. "You have
been gone. For years. Ever since Mom got sick." She stopped and glared
at him. Her chest felt tight, like she could barely breath. "How could you
let her die like that?"

Phillip inhaled sharply. He took off his glasses.

Sweat beaded on Melody's forehead. Her freckles burned. "All you do
is work. All you care about is your god-damned grad students and your
papers and..." Melody paused. She felt like a submarine about to fire off
a nuclear missile. "And who the fuck is Lydia, Dad? Lydia, your new heart
throb?" Melody glared.

Phillip gasped.

Melody stopped. She looked carefully at her father, his face creased in
the shadows, suddenly pale, eyes shut tight, lips rigid. She squinted in the
dusky light. *He is sleeping with her...Oh god, are those tears?*

His chest shuddered, and he sputtered in a whisper. "Mel honey, Mom
had cancer, real bad. The doctors tried to save her." He dragged his fist
across his damp eyelids. "There wasn't much I could do, besides just be
there for her and love her to the very end. I'm sorry, sweetheart. I'm so,
so very sorry."

"And?"

"I just wanted to protect you."

"Protect me? You just pushed me off the dock without a boat. Without
a fucking life preserver."

"I just wanted your life to be..."

"To be what?"

"To be normal."

"Normal? There was nothing normal about my life. Mom shrinking away until she was…just a skeleton. All those poisonous chemo drugs. She didn't even have eyelashes Dad."

"Mel."

"You were so absent. I needed you to catch me. Hold me. Comfort me. Talk to me. Do you even know how to do that?" Melody stopped pacing and leaned across the table. "And speaking of comfort, who the hell is Lydia?"

Her father took a very deep breath and looked up into the trees, avoiding her gaze. "Okay, okay," he nodded. "Lydia is…" He turned to meet Melody's fierce stare. "An old flame, back in school, college. I didn't know she would be here. Really."

"Are you like dating her or something? Do you love her? Is she going to move in with us? Is she going to be the New Mother? Is that why you came here?" Melody almost shouted, "You can't replace Mom, you know. You can't replace her." The thought of Lydia invading her house. *Ugh*, she felt like puking. "How could you betray Mom like that?"

"Mel, honey. Listen to me. No one can replace Mom."

A flood burst inside Melody's chest. Her ribs ached from the explosion. Wet tears dripped down her cheeks. She couldn't breathe. She grabbed her bracelet and held on.

"Losing your mom was so painful. I couldn't bear it." Phillip shuddered again. "I tried to be there for you. I didn't know what to do…how to be a mother/father to you." He wiped his dripping nose with his hand. "Clearly," he looked directly at her. "I failed."

Phillip shook his head. "My hurt was …too much. The whole thing felt so unfair. To everybody…especially you." He stared up into the olive tree and pursed his lips together, his Adams apple bouncing up and down as he swallowed, holding back tears. "I guess I was just living in unfathomable pain, day to day. I could barely keep my head above water."

He ground his hands together and looked directly at his daughter. "And now I'm afraid I'm gonna lose you too." Phillip sobbed quietly. "I'm really scared."

Melody sat down.

"You know, Mel, like you, I'm lonely, I'm a lonely person. I know it's hard for you to imagine this, but our lives are not over, sweetheart. I need this pain to quiet down inside me. I need some loving too."

Melody turned away.

"You're all I've really got, Mel. I love you. I know you don't believe me, but I really do." He pulled out a handkerchief and wiped his nose, looking directly into her eyes. "Please let me into your fortress." Phillip straightened his back and held his hand out cautiously. "It's lonesome out here in the cold."

Melody stared at her father, her whole body shaking. She stood up, bit her lip, and rolled her bracelet over her wrist again and again. She rocked back and forth on her heels and eyed the old olive tree, so sturdy and twisted. *A survivor.*

In the shadows of the trees, she saw her mom's face, pale and shaky, lips dry. Melody sitting on her bed, her father on the opposite side. Her mom reaching out to each of them with her thin, veiny hands. "Take good care of each other. Okay?" The shadows faded.

All the disappointment and loss, rage and unending grief, spread out on the table between Melody and her father. She thought about Dov's heaving body pressing against her, the checkpoints, refugee camps and soldiers, the scar on Mahmoud's arm. The kindness of strangers. The embrace of Yaz's family. She heard Yasmina's voice, "Be strong and be kind."

Melody walked slowly toward her Dad, her feet crunching on the dry leaves and twigs, and took his hand, gently but firmly. It felt warm and wet from sweat. "Okay, Dad. No promises. No bullshit. Let's try again."

Chapter Thirty-Two

LOST AND FOUND

MELODY CRAWLED INTO BED, HOURS AFTER everyone had gone to sleep. She heard the muffled sounds of her father shuffling out of the bathroom. Otherwise the house was quiet, except for the night music of soft breathing, snorts, and snores, the occasional fart and rustle of sheets. She sat up in her bed, leaning against her pillow, knees bent, a blanket pulled over her head and pointed her cellphone light at her notebook. She flipped through the pages with one hand, reading through her lists and poems. Khulood's creased phone number fell on the sheet. She grabbed the scrap of paper and kissed it.

Melody picked up her pen, balancing her notebook on her knees.

Page eight

Walls

People build walls out of pain,
Nations build walls out of fear,
Are we safer or ghettoized?
Are we protected
Or imprisoned?

The blanket slipped down to her shoulders, and Melody turned her cellphone light into the sheet, the room suddenly dark. A sliver of moonlight pierced through the window. She hugged her knees to her chest and stared at the ray of shimmery light. She smiled. A message from the moon goddess? Yasmina coughed and turned in bed. Melody pulled the blanket back over her head and reached for her pen.

Page nine

THE FOREVER LEFT BEHINDS

1. *Black hole in my heart*
2. *Orphan girl*
3. *Smoking weed, ever ever!!!*
4. *Private wars*
5. *Fighting alone*
6. *Hating Dad's clothes*
7. *Hating Dad*
8. *Powerlessness*
9. *Silence*

She turned the page and stopped, staring into the semi-darkness at the rose on her wrist, the swooping stem sloping into M-O-M, the jagged scars hidden by curling leaves. Her heart thumped against her chest. She bit her lip a few times, nibbled on one of her fingernails, and curled over her notebook, hand trembling.

Page nine

Mom,
I'm gonna be okay.
I think Daddy loves me,
even when he doesn't know how to tell me.
Even when I think he does stupid things.
I think I can love him back,
even when I have a wildfire burning inside.

(Which is, after all, every day.)

For so long we've been
orbiting our separate planets of grief.

I love Yaz.
And maybe even Aaron,
Because my friends hold me close,

black fingernails, torn jeans, F bombs and all,
listen to me, worry about me,
while I'm balancing on this tightrope which is my life,
toes curled, arms flung out, wobbling, trying not to scream.

Knowing there is a safety net down there,
somewhere,
that will hold me.
Knowing that everyone else is dancing,
on their own tightropes, just like me.

Melody stretched out her legs and let the blanket fall from her head. Her phone glowed against the bedspread. She looked at Yasmina, curled up, a bit of drool staining her pillowcase, her hair coursing across the puffs and crevices of the bed. On the other side, Rana moaned quietly while Huda's arm drooped over the edge of her mattress as if she were grabbing something in her sleep. A sultry breeze meandered through the open window, layered with the fragrance of jasmine and dusty summer heat.

Melody slunk down and pulled the blanket over her head again, cocooned. *I so want to be done with Angry, Lonely, Confused.* She felt a knot in her chest loosening and rubbed her nose ring.

Mom,
somewhere, (wherever you are),
I know you are spinning silky webs to catch me,
like a giant celestial spider.
and I feel you, holding me tight.

I know you never meant to leave me.
Life can really suck suck suck.

Melody stopped, tapped her pen on her bracelet for a minute. She crossed out the last line.

I know you never meant to leave me.
~~Life can really suck suck suck.~~
I will never really understand
that combo of bad luck, ill fate, unfairness,

that overturned our lives.

After all the wailing and weeping,
I want to be washed free of my rage.

Melody felt her eyes brimming, heavy with accumulated sorrow and regret. She wiped her face with the back of her hand and snuffled softly.

My job is to keep dancing on that tight rope,
Tripping, falling,
scrambling back up.
Feeling your presence,
your guiding hand,
wherever I am.

Chapter Thirty-Three

THE BUTTERED BISCUIT

MELODY SQUIRTED KETCHUP ON HER CHEESEBURGER and moved The Buttered Biscuit menu away from any unexpected airborne condiments. Yasmina leaned her back against the diner window, stretching her legs across the faux leather seat, a plate of apple pie balanced on her knees. The booth was permeated with the smells of old coffee and dried maple syrup.

"Man, the fries in Palestine were soooo good. What's the secret Yaz?"

Yasmina shrugged. "Can't you see, I'm eating apple pie?" She licked her fingers. "I'm staying in the present. It's very calming."

"So…you're as American as apple…"

"Pie. That's right." She whisked her hand into the air. "I can't think about fries."

"Too French?"

"Mais oui." Yasmina picked at the crumbling crust. She tossed a piece in her mouth and bent her knees, readjusting her plate. "But seriously Mel, I thought we were talking about my college essay."

"Sorry Yaz, I'm so easily distracted by red meat." Melody grinned. "Plus, I don't want you to go. Should I throw my body across the table? Into an oncoming train filled with college applications?"

"You're hopeless," she laughed. "Besides, they're all online."

"If you try to go to some faraway college, I'm gonna tie you to my bed. Put Cheddar on guard duty. What's wrong with staying here?" Melody stopped and bit her lip. "Okay, okay," she frowned and made a sad face. "Tell me more. Your essay sounds like some weird summer vacation story."

"Yeah, just the usual." Yasmina gave Melody an exaggerated wink. Her voice got low and gravelly, and she crunched her eyebrows together. "What I Did on My Summer Vacation by Yasmina Khdour: Waited at checkpoints for hours. Stared down Israeli soldiers with humongous guns. Helped my uncle with his wound dressings. Resisted my charming, ever-hopeful grandmother's attempts to marry me off. Stuffed eggplants. Please let me into your college. Sincerely yours. A typical American girl. The end."

"Just your average summer vacation." Melody laughed.

"Seriously Mel." Melody felt Yasmina go all urgent and somber. She braced herself and tugged at her baseball cap. "I really want to write about my uncle, what it means to be a journalist in occupied territory. That kind of daily bravery and stubbornness." Yasmina took another bite of pie and chewed slowly. "And then his injury, how he faced it. How he inspired me." Yasmina shook her head up and down like she was launching these ideas into the airways. Testing them out.

"That's pretty brave, Yaz, being so public about your Palestinian-ness. Especially in this crazy country where so many people are afraid of women wearing hijabs." She chomped a fry. "And A-rabs in general."

Yasmina sat up straight, dropping pie crumbs all over her jeans. "Well, that's who I am. Right?"

Melody nodded.

"Can I join you guys?" Aaron leaned on the end of the table, his fingers tapping on the speckled Formica. "I thought you two might be here, usual spot." His kippah was flipping off the back of his head.

Melody slid over. "Sure, want some fries?" Aaron glided in, like a plane coming in for landing, as his kippah tumbled down his back. He grabbed it, dropped it into the tangle of his hair, pushed his back against the bench, and pressed his leg against Melody. She felt a warm electric jolt in her thigh. She willed her brain to ignore the low-level fireworks. "Are you okay? You look really upset."

Yasmina swiveled and dropped her legs onto the floor, dusting off her lap. She stared at Aaron. "Do you need some pie?"

Aaron shook his head, no. He reached for the menu.

"Come on, Aaron," Melody said. "You're gonna order a Coke, that's all you ever order. Nothing else here is kosher enough for you. What's going on?"

Aaron fiddled with the menu. Melody nudged him with her knee. "Aaron?"

"I had a fight with my dad." He rubbed the back of his neck.

Yasmina's eyebrows shot up. "About?"

Aaron exhaled loudly. "I showed him the photos you sent, Mel. From Judea, I mean from the West Bank. You know the checkpoints and the refugee camp and the marketplace in Hebron." His voice cracked. "And my cousin." He stared out the plate glass window, unfocused, his eyebrows crunched together, his cheek dimpling.

"You did?" Melody inched away from him and pivoted to get a better look. "And…"

He turned to her. "It wasn't pretty. I mean I'm still not sure where I stand on all this, but I trust you. You saw what you saw. Yaz's family sounds just like…regular nice people. They were really nice to you. They're living in a hard place."

"I'm glad you can see that," said Yasmina.

Aaron rubbed his nose and caught his breath. "And my dad, he went all ballistic about Arab terrorists killing Jews and all the Holocaust stuff and Iran and how we need a safe place. You can't imagine."

"Oh, I think I can," said Yasmina, playing with the edges of her hijab.

"Me too." Melody nodded. "What did you say?"

"He said you were brainwashed. I, I just told him I wanted to talk about it, what you two told me. That I thought it might be good to maybe think about another perspective. But man, he got really mad. Kind of defensive. Accused me of going over to the other side."

"Really?" Melody patted his hand. "Look Aaron. If Yaz and me are the other side, how bad could it be?"

Aaron smiled and wobbled his head as if he were considering agreeing.

"I got a new theory, Aaron. Our lives are like tightropes." Melody stretched her fists apart as if holding a rope over the table. "And we're just all trying not to fall off." She twisted her body back and forth. "But we will."

"That's for sure. I really respect my dad. I just don't know what to do."

Melody held her imaginary rope tight. "But then we get back up. You know, like that Beatle's song my mom loved, the one about a little help from your friends."

Aaron's face relaxed. Melody put her hands back on the table, and Aaron reached over and squeezed her little finger. She felt like purring, but managed to put a shy smile on her face.

Yasmina sank back into her seat. "You guys." She turned to see the waitress arrive.

"The usual, hon? Coke? No ice?"

Aaron tilted his head, his dimple deepening. "What are the biscuits made of? Butter and flour?"

The waitress nodded. "Trade secret, but I'll admit to sugar, eggs, and baking powder."

"And salt?" Melody chimed in.

The waitress grinned. "Salt. Makes everything taste better."

Aaron inhaled loudly. "I'll have a biscuit too. Maple syrup on the side."

"Wow." Melody gave his little finger a gentle squeeze.

An orange-bellied towhee flitted across the window, perched on a branch, and stared directly into the diner. Melody could have sworn the bird winked at her.

GLOSSARY

Aba: (Hebrew) father

Abaya: (Arabic) loose robe-like dress worn by many women in the Muslim world, head, hands, and feet exposed

Aliyah: (Hebrew) Jewish immigration to Israel, implies a spiritual journey

Baba ganoush: (Arabic) finely chopped roasted eggplant, olive oil, lemon juice, various seasonings, and tahini

Basbousa: (Arabic) dessert made of semolina flour drenched in simple syrup

Foul: (Arabic) crushed fava beans, lemon juice, garlic, and olive oil

G-D, god: (English) religious Jews are not allowed to say the Lord's name and will often hyphenate when writing, while secular Jews often write the name as pronounced, sometimes without capitalization

Habibti: (Arabic) sweetheart (female)

Hashem: (Hebrew) term for G-d, literally means "the name," as religious Jews are forbidden to say G-d's name casually or in vain, this is one of several accepted workarounds

Hassidim: (Hebrew) a branch of very traditional, devout Orthodox Jews, divided into sects, each following a particular rabbi as their spiritual leader

Hijab: (Arabic) headscarf worn by Muslim women

IDF: (English) Israeli Defense Force

Ima: (Hebrew) mother

Intifada: (Arabic) popular uprising, rebellion, resistance movement

Ka'ek: (Arabic) ring shaped crusty bread covered in sesame seeds

Kanafeh: (Arabic) pastry made of cheese and pistachios

Kippah: (Hebrew) brimless cap traditionally worn by Orthodox Jewish men, in Reform temples may also be worn by women

Ledaber anglit?: (Hebrew) Speak English?

Lo: (Hebrew) no

Mah zey: (Hebrew) What's that?

Makhluta: (Arabic) mix of roasted, salted nuts

Maqluba: (Arabic) chicken, vegetable, and rice dish, served upside down

Marhaba: (Arabic) common greeting, hello, welcome

Mezuzah: (Hebrew) tiny piece of parchment containing a prayer, placed in a decorative case, and nailed to the doorposts in a Jewish home

Nargileh: (Arabic) water pipe for smoking flavored tobacco, also called hookah

Oud: (Arabic) lute-like, plucked string instrument

Schnitzel: (English, German) thinly sliced chicken or turkey dipped in egg, bread crumbs, spices, and fried

Shawarma: (Arabic) thin sliced meat cooked on a rotisserie

Sherut: (Hebrew) shared taxi used in Israel

Sh'ma Yisra'el, Adonai eloheinu, Adonai 'ehad: (Hebrew) central Jewish prayer, Hear, O Israel: the Lord is our God, the Lord is one, found in Deuteronomy

Sitti: (Arabic) grandmother

Slicha, gveret: (Hebrew) Sorry, miss

Sumac: (English) commonly used spice in Middle Eastern cooking, made from ground up sumac berries

Tablah: (Arabic) hand drum

Tabbouleh: (Arabic) Middle Eastern salad made mostly of finely chopped parsley, with tomatoes, mint, onion, bulgur, and seasoned with olive oil, lemon juice

Toda: (Hebrew) thank you

Tzadik: (Hebrew) righteous person

Tzitzit: (Hebrew) knotted fringes or tassels, part of a tallit (ceremonial shawl) or an undergarment worn by religious Jewish men and boys

Um: (Arabic) mother of

Yalla: (Arabic) come on, let's go, hurry up, all right, also adopted by Hebrew speaking Israelis

Yeshiva: (Hebrew) traditional Jewish school focused on the study of Rabbinic literature (Torah, Talmud, Jewish law, and philosophy)

Zaatar: (Arabic) commonly used spice of dried sumac, thyme, and toasted sesame seeds

Acknowledgements

W RITING A NOVEL IS OFTEN A LONG AND LONELY process that was made possible for me by a supportive and loving community. With appreciation and gratitude, I want to thank all the folks who read and critiqued this book and offered me encouragement and good advice. In particular, amongst friends and family, a major thank you to Lubna Alzaroo, Emma Klein, Jessie Maag, Jen Marlowe, and Jaylyn Olivo.

I have also been lucky to work with Lauren Clark, Michelle Griskey, Severine Pathak, and Mary Sloat, members of my trusty, supportive, and thoughtful writing critique group.

Much of this novel comes from a lifetime of experiences working with patients as an ob-gyn and doing health and human rights work in Israel/Palestine. I am grateful to every person who has shared their troubles, victories, and stories with me, both in the US and the Middle East.

Lastly, a big thank you to Scott Davis who felt this was a narrative worthy of publishing.

Brief excerpts in the novel from the "Lonely Planet" and the guide in Jerusalem are based on the travel book, "Lonely Planet: Israel & the Palestinian Territories," by Daniel Robinson, Orlando Crowcroft, Anita Isalska, Dan Savery Raz, Jenny Walker, published by Lonely Planet Global Limited, July 2018.

CUNE PRESS WAS FOUNDED in 1994 to publish thoughtful writing of public importance. Our name is derived from "cuneiform." (In Latin *cuni* means "wedge.")

In the ancient Near East the development of cuneiform script—simpler and more adaptable than hieroglyphics—enabled a large class of merchants and landowners to become literate. Clay tablets inscribed with wedge-shaped stylus marks made possible a broad inter-meshing of individual efforts in trade and commerce.

Cuneiform enabled scholarship to exist, art to flower, and created what historians define as the world's first civilization. When the Phoenicians developed their sound-based alphabet, they expressed it in cuneiform.

The idea of Cune Press is the democratization of learning, the faith that rarefied ideas—pulled from dusty pedestals and displayed in the streets—can transform the lives of ordinary people. And it is the conviction that ordinary people, trusted with the most precious gifts of civilization, will give our culture elasticity and depth—a necessity if we are to survive in a time of rapid change.

ALICE ROTHCHILD is a physician, author, and filmmaker who loves storytelling that pushes boundaries and engages us in unexpected conversations. She practiced ob-gyn for almost 40 years and served as Assistant Professor of Obstetrics and Gynecology, Harvard Medical School. She writes and lectures widely, is the author of *Broken Promises, Broken Dreams: Stories of Jewish and Palestinian Trauma and Resilience* (translated into German and Hebrew); *On the Brink: Israel and Palestine on the Eve of the 2014 Gaza Invasion*; and *Condition Critical: Life and Death in Israel/Palestine* and she has contributed to a number of anthologies and poetry journals. She directed a documentary film, Voices Across the Divide and is a mentor for We Are Not Numbers, a program that supports young writers in Gaza. She received Boston Magazine's Best of Boston's Women Doctors Award, was named in Feminists Who Changed America 1963-1975, had her portrait painted for Robert Shetterly's Americans Who Tell the Truth, and was named a Peace Pioneer by the American Jewish Peace Archive.

Website www.alicerothchildbooks.com
Facebook https://www.facebook.com/alicerothchildmd
Twitter https://twitter.com/alicerothchild
Instagram https://www.instagram.com/alicerothchild/

CPSIA information can be obtained
at www.ICGtesting.com
Printed in the USA
LVHW052328290123
738188LV00003B/709